THE
MORONI
CODE

THE
MORONI
CODE

JACK LYON

DESERET
BOOK

SALT LAKE CITY, UTAH

Image of "Caractors" transcript on pages 21, 186, and cover from Ariel L. Crowley, "The Anthon Transcript," in *Improvement Era,* February 1942, 77.

Photograph of Big Dipper on page 38 used courtesy of Isaac Taylor.

Library of Congress Cataloging-in-Publication Data

Lyon, Jack M.
  The Moroni code / Jack Lyon.
    p. cm.
  ISBN-13: 978-1-59038-810-5 (pbk.)
  1. Mormons—Fiction. 2. Government investigators—Fiction.
3. Extortion—Fiction. I. Title.
  PS3612.Y559M67 2007
  813'.6—dc22   2007025653

Printed in the United States of America
Publishers Printing, Salt Lake City, UT

10   9   8   7   6   5   4   3   2   1

For Anne, with love

This book is a *novel,* a work of fiction; it is not intended to be a work of scholarship. Nevertheless, with one exception, all of the quotations, documents, and artifacts mentioned in this book are real, including the transcript of Book of Mormon characters.

PROLOGUE

꙳ ≋ ⼂

The big man trudged through the fallen leaves, his shoulders aching from the weight of his pack. Where was he going to hide these things? And how? They had to be protected. But they also had to be found—eventually. He smiled grimly. *God will take care of that.*

A chill wind rattled through the maples and birch trees, forcing him to pick up his pace. As he reached the hill, he decided to go clear to the top—but that meant climbing. He trudged on—and up—his pack biting into his back.

As he neared the summit, he unstrapped his load and sat on a large, slightly rounded stone, resting for several minutes. He was exhausted. *Why not right here?* he thought.

After a few more moments of rest, he found a smaller stone that would work for a scraper, then loosened the dark earth just downhill from the large one. He moved the earth aside, dug deeper, then moved more aside, until finally the hole was the size he needed. He carefully squared off the sides and bottom and then went looking for more stones, which were scattered in profusion about the hillside. Higher up, he found exactly what he was looking for, and, one at a time, he lugged five large, flat stones back to the hole.

Finding that the stones were a bit too big, he scraped the hole's sides until he could fit one of the stones into the bottom. Then, reaching into his pack, he located a leather pouch filled with a sticky black substance—pitch. This he packed along the edges of the bottom stone, then placed the other four stones on their sides into the tarry sludge, adding additional pitch to form a watertight stone box inside the hole.

Finally, he laid two more stones crosswise on the bottom, placed the breastplate facedown on top of them, formed three pillars from the remaining pitch, and pushed them down onto the concave back of the breastplate. Then he slept.

The next day, he put the plates into the box, resting them on the pillars. Near them he laid the other remaining treasures of his people, including the precious Interpreters. Finally, he pushed the large, rounded stone until it completely covered the box, burying its contents in darkness, waiting for another prophet, another time.

PART ONE

CHAPTER 1

After dinner, David Hunter was finally in his bedroom, alone. His parents were oblivious, watching TV, so he lay down on his bed in the darkness, switched on the light on his nightstand, and pulled the paperback book out from under the mattress. He had just started to read when he heard his father coming up the stairs. He managed to shove the book under his pillow just as his father pushed in the door.

"What are you doing, David?"

"Just thinking—about things."

"I see. What's that sticking out from under your pillow?"

"What? Dad—"

David's father pulled out the small, dark-blue book, then looked at his son with dismay.

"The Book of Mormon? You're reading the Book of Mormon?"

David gestured feebly. "It's homework, Dad. It's for seminary."

His father scowled. "You shouldn't be taking seminary."

"I like it. It's interesting."

David's father sighed and sat on the corner of the bed. "You're sixteen years old. It's time you grew up. 'When I was a child, I spake as a child, I understood as a child, I thought as a child: but when I became a man, I put away childish things.' Don't they teach you that in seminary?"

"I don't know, Dad. I—"

"David, listen. The Book of Mormon is full of mistakes—spelling errors, grammar errors, all kinds of things."

"That's your thing, Dad. I don't care about that stuff."

"You should. Look, the book is supposed to be inspired—dictated by God, or whatever. Don't you think God should be able to spell?"

"Yeah."

"Well then?"

"I don't know. Maybe if I read it, I'll find out. Isn't that what you're always saying—that we should think things out for ourselves?"

His father smiled thinly. "Well, you've got me there."

"Don't worry, Dad. I'll read it to find out, okay? It doesn't mean I'm going on a mission or anything like that."

"All right. Fine. Just try to keep a critical mind. Don't get sucked in too easily. These people can be very convincing."

"I know. I'll be careful."

After his dad left, David read for a few more minutes. He liked finding connections in the text, seeing the subtle patterns in the narrative—something he'd always been good at. But his thoughts kept getting in the way. Finally, he put the book on his nightstand and stared at the ceiling. Maybe his dad had a point. Why *did* the book have mistakes, anyway?

CHAPTER 2

꙳ ≋ ꙴ V

After the funeral, the whole family came back to the house in Midvale and sat around the living room, which now seemed to carry reminders of Grandpa Woodman in every corner—his prized collection of nautical etchings, the stack of early Mormon books on his side table, and, most of all, his big brown recliner, where no one seemed willing to sit. The family talked and reminisced until late into the night, when eventually people started drifting out the big front door into the cool autumn air, heading for home.

David, now out of college and working for the FBI, was getting ready to leave—back to his apartment in downtown Salt Lake City—when his grandmother caught his arm. "Don't go yet," she said.

"Oh, Grandma, I really need to get home. I've got to get some sleep before I fall over."

"It'll just take a minute. There's something your grandfather wanted you to have." She put her hand on his cheek. "You're so much like him, you know, especially when he was young—tall, dark, and handsome, with the same curiosity about everything under the sun." She sighed and patted his hand. "Come see what he left you—it's not much, I'm afraid." And she led him back to his grandfather's study, where she opened a drawer of the old rolltop desk and pulled out a small, white cardboard box—the kind jewelry might come in. "These are some of your grandpa's old tie tacks," she said. "There's a diamond one in here somewhere; I know he'd love it if you wore it once in a while. But here's the really valuable thing." She pulled out a faded slip of paper. "This belonged to your great-great-grandfather. He made it when he was in Kirtland, Ohio, with the Prophet Joseph Smith."

David took the paper, which was covered with strange symbols.

"What is it?" he said.

"It's a copy of characters from the gold plates."

"Really?"

"That's what your grandfather always said. Look here on the back." She reached out with her thin fingers and turned the paper over.

> Copied by my own hand from caractors shown by Martin Harris to Prof. Anthon, in fulfillment of Prophisy, Isai. 29. Joseph Woodman, Kirtland, 1834.

"Wow." He turned the paper back over, examining the lines one by one. "Why is this one character circled?"

"You'd have to ask your grandpa," she said. Then she choked up. "And now you can't."

David put his arms around his grandmother's frail shoulders, which shook as she cried, her cheek against his chest.

Finally, her sobs subsided. But now David was having a hard time keeping his composure.

"Grandma?"

"Yes, David?"

His voice caught. "Will we ever see Grandpa again?"

She took his large hands in her small ones. "Oh, my dear one. Don't you know?"

"I've *never* known, Grandma. You must understand that." Tears filled his eyes.

"Oh, that father of yours."

"I love him, Grandma. He's taught me lots of good things."

"Of course he has, dear. But he's discouraged you from learning the most important thing: that the gospel is true. And that's something no one else can teach you."

David didn't know what to say. On his mother's insistence, he'd been baptized when he turned eight, and he'd been active most of his life. But he'd never gained a testimony, never known that the Church was true. And as he'd grown older, he'd had serious questions about Church history and doctrine—something that had been fed by his dad.

His grandmother eyed David intently. "You're not just your father's son, you know. You have your grandfather's blood running through your veins. And mine." Her eyes twinkled. "You *need* to find out."

"Okay, Grandma," he said. "I'll try."

"Good," she said. "I'll expect a full report." And she kissed him on the cheek.

MANCHESTER, NEW YORK, OCTOBER, 1828

꙳ ≋ ⼻

That was a delicious meal, Mrs. Smith." Oliver Cowdery pushed himself back from the table.

"Thank you, Mr. Cowdery. I'm glad you enjoyed it. You look as though you could use a little fattening up."

Oliver laughed. The new teacher for the village school, he'd been boarding with Joseph Smith Sr. and his wife, Lucy, for two weeks now. He'd tried to ask them about the "gold bible" he'd heard so much about, but so far they'd been unwilling to say anything about it.

"Mr. Smith," Oliver said cautiously, "do you hear any news from your namesake?"

The older man threw up his hands. "You are persistent, Mr. Cowdery, very persistent, I must say. Otherwise, you seem a decent enough young man."

"Thank you, sir. I do apologize. But I feel strongly that there is truth in the stories being noised abroad."

Joseph glanced at his wife, Lucy, who nodded. "Very well, then, since you are not inclined to ridicule. Yes, our son Joseph was in truth visited by an angel, who told him the location of the plates of gold. Upon these plates is an ancient record, the history of the former inhabitants of this continent, and my son has obtained the plates and is under obligation from God to translate them."

Oliver looked at the old man intently. "I have been praying about this, and I feel impressed that I shall yet have the privilege of writing for your son—of assisting in the translation, if he will have me."

"And your contract for teaching?"

Oliver looked down. "In the spring, after school is finished, I will be free."

"Our son Samuel will be traveling to Harmony in the spring. I'm sure he'd be happy to have a companion. And Joseph would be glad of the help."

Oliver drew himself up to his full height of five feet five inches. His dark eyes were piercing. "I believe it is God's will that I go. And if there is a work for me to do in this thing, I am determined to attend to it."

"Then God bless you, Mr. Cowdery." Mr. Smith put his hand on the little man's shoulder. "And may his will be done."

CHAPTER 3

꜀꜀ ꜀꜀ ꜀꜀ V

Thornton Price, a librarian and archivist for the LDS Church Historical Department, liked strolling around downtown Salt Lake City during his lunch hour, and today he was walking east on 200 South. The day was sunny but cold, even for November, and he turned up the collar of his dress coat, frowning at the street's seediness—the dilapidated bar, the magazine store with its vulgar window display, the homeless man with his ragged coat and shopping cart. But right now he was out for business, not pleasure. As he turned the corner, he saw the sign he was looking for:

PITT BROTHERS RARE BOOKS AND MANUSCRIPTS
MORMON DOCUMENTS—WESTERN AMERICANA

Stopping to straighten his tie, he looked himself over in the glass front door, then ran his fingers through his meticulously trimmed blond hair. As he opened the door, a small brass bell announced his entrance, and the smell of dust and paper met his nostrils.

Seth Pitt came out from the back room, carrying a stack of books. "Hi, Thornton," he said.

"Hello, Seth. Got anything new?" Seth always made Thornton a little uneasy, with his greasy black ponytail and garish tattoos. Thornton was vaguely aware of problems in

Seth's past—as a young man he'd spent time in prison. Fraud, maybe? And rumor had it that he'd once killed a man—manslaughter? He'd served his time, though, and had evidently cleaned up his act. He was certainly cordial enough to Thornton. He was also the brains of the bookstore operation—a real wheeler-dealer, always ready to make a buck.

Seth put the books down on the counter. "Here's a nice copy of *Brigham Young at Home,* inscribed by his daughter."

"No, thanks," Thornton said. "Listen, is Sonny here?" He adjusted his glasses.

"He went out for a bite to eat. Should be back in just a few."

"All right. Okay if I wait?"

"Sure. Check out our latest manuscript display." Seth waved his hand toward a glass display case near the door.

"Thanks." Thornton moved over to the case and peered down at the carefully arranged documents. Each one was a letter signed by a president of the Church, starting with Joseph Smith and ending with the current prophet, Grant W. Iverson. "Wow," he said. "Very nice."

"Thanks. It took some doing to get the complete collection. The early guys are pretty hard to find. And the later guys kept their cards pretty close to the vest." He laughed, his ponytail bobbing up and down.

Then the brass bell jingled, and Sonny came rolling in, breathing heavily, his big stomach peeking out from his untucked shirt. He didn't look like much, but Thornton knew that if Seth was the businessman, Sonny was the history buff. He could appraise an old book almost at a glance.

"Hey, Thornton. What's up?"

"Nothing, really. I was wondering if you two would be interested in some Joseph Smith documents I've stumbled onto."

"Sure," Sonny said. "The Church doesn't want them?"

"I came across these on my personal time."

"Does that make a difference?" Sonny laughed.

"Of course it makes a difference. Just because it's my job to find historical documents doesn't mean the Church owns me."

Sonny feigned sympathy. "No, no, of course not."

"Where did you find the documents?"

"Actually, they belong to my great-aunt. She had ancestors in Kirtland."

"Okay."

"So here's the deal. I'll bring in the documents, one at a time, and I won't talk to anybody else. In return, though, you'll need to pay me top dollar. If you're not interested, I have other contacts—"

"Don't worry, we're interested. How many documents are we talking about?"

"Well . . . I'm not sure."

"Really."

"I haven't actually got them yet. I wanted to check around first—with you and others."

"Sure."

"And, well, I need money to buy them from my aunt. She's not just going to give them to me."

"Oh, I see. How much do you need?"

Thornton swallowed. "Twenty thousand dollars should do it. She doesn't know it, but the documents are worth ten times that much—maybe a lot more." He took a deep breath. "I'd prefer cash."

Sonny looked at his brother and winked. "Gee, Seth, that's not much at all. What do you think?"

"You've got to be kidding. There's no way we could loan you that kind of money. We don't *have* that kind of money."

Thornton pulled some documents out of his coat pocket. "For security, I could give you these right now, from my own collection. This one is a letter from Brigham Young about the federal army coming to Salt Lake. And this one"—Thornton smiled—"well, this one is a letter from Emma Smith to her mother."

Sonny took the documents and peered closely at them, bringing each one only inches from his nose. He felt the texture of the paper between his thumb and fingers, held them up to the light. Finally he nodded at Seth.

"Okay," Seth said. "We could probably loan you five thousand dollars."

"How am I supposed to buy a document collection with five thousand dollars?"

"Uh, well, one at a time. You said that's how you'd be bringing them in."

Thornton thought for a moment. "All right. That would probably work."

"You bring us a Joseph Smith document—a really good one—and we'll give you more. But these documents here are for security; the five thousand is a loan. And don't forget, Thornton—we know where you live."

The brothers laughed. Then Seth went into the back room to open the safe.

CHAPTER 4

H ello, dear," Thornton called. "I'm home." He looked around the spacious living room, with its hardwood floor, Oriental carpet, and lush custom draperies, feeling his usual flash of pride in the room's design—his own. Then he caught the smell of roast beef coming from the kitchen. He laid his briefcase on the large, red-leather sofa and hung his dress coat in the closet.

Tamara, Thornton's wife, came out of the bedroom. "Oh, Thornton. Can't you ever be on time? We're having the Andersons over for dinner. Did you forget?"

"I'm sorry. I've been a little preoccupied lately."

"I've noticed." She took off his jacket and tie and kissed him on the cheek.

"You smell good," he said. "And you look terrific." She was wearing her "little black dress," accented by the string of pearls—real ones—he'd given her for Christmas; her dark-brown hair was pulled back from her face to show off the matching earrings.

"Why don't you go freshen up? Put on a clean shirt and tie. The Andersons will be here any minute."

"All right." He turned to leave, then paused. "Did you straighten out that problem with the mortgage payment?"

"I paid it with money from a credit card."

"Tamara, you know we can't keep doing that." He fingered his wedding ring. "It's robbing Peter to pay Paul. If we keep it up, we're bound to lose the house."

"Isn't there something you can do about that?"

"We've talked about this before. If you could just be a little more careful—"

Her dark eyes flashed. "I'm not going to be careful—and we've talked about *that* before. You told me when we got married that you'd take care of me the way my parents had—and you knew what that meant."

"I still do," he said. "But you don't understand what it means to come from a middle-class family. Everything I have, I've had to work for. It's not easy, you know."

Tamara put her hand on his shoulder. "I know. But you can do it, Thornton. I've always known that. I didn't *want* to marry someone who had everything handed to him." She smiled. "You're a go-getter. That's one of the things I love about you."

"I'll be getting a raise next month," he said.

"And what about that promotion?"

"I'm working on it. But Daniel isn't moving out of that position any time soon."

"That's one of the problems with working for the Church—nobody ever leaves. Maybe you can make him look bad." She smiled, her perfect teeth matching her pearls.

"I can't believe you'd say something like that."

She threw up her hands. "Oh, like everybody at the Church Office Building is just full of goodness and light. They've been taking advantage of you for years."

"Dear, you know that's not true. And besides, I'm working on a new business arrangement—on the side."

"What? What business arrangement?"

"I can't tell you about it yet. But it's already starting to pay off. Look." He opened his briefcase and pulled out the sheaf of bills.

"How in the world . . ."

"I'll explain when things are further along. There'll be more where this came from."

She threw her arms around his neck and kissed him over and over. Then she paused. "You're not doing anything illegal, are you?"

"Of course not. What a thing to say!"

"I always knew you had it in you," she said. "I always knew."

And for a long moment, he kissed her back.

CHAPTER 5

⋝ ≋ ⊣ ∨

David was happy to leave the FBI office and go for a brisk walk through downtown Salt Lake City. He enjoyed his work as a special agent—a linguist, specializing in cryptography—but he worked on other kinds of cases too, sometimes out in the field, and dealing with sex predators and terrorist suspects was not exactly uplifting. Sometimes, schedule permitting, he just had to get away. And besides, winter was all but done, and the unseasonably beautiful March weather had been calling him all morning from his office window. It was the perfect day to walk over to the Church Office Building to see what he could learn about the document he'd inherited from his grandfather—something he'd been putting off for too long.

As he approached the building, some lettering on the big glass windows—"Historical Library"—pointed him to a revolving door on the right, which made a loud whooshing sound as he entered. He admired the expansive lobby, with its comfortably arranged seating and its giant mural of Jesus and the apostles on the east wall. *Go ye into all the world,* he thought. A security guard at the library entrance checked his identification and had him sign in—"Name and time, name and time."

As he approached the reference desk, he noticed a young

woman talking on the phone. Covering the mouthpiece with her hand, she whispered, "I'll be right with you."

David nodded and leaned on the counter, taking the opportunity to admire her blonde curls and sparkling blue eyes—not exactly the standard picture of a librarian. He'd noticed other women—out in the lobby—who were dressed in a variety of fabrics and colors but all in what appeared to be some sort of uniform—an ankle-length skirt, a blouse buttoned to the chin, and a jacket. But this young woman was wearing a frilly pink dress—a rather nice change, David thought.

Just then she hung up the phone and smiled, warming David clear to his toes. "May I help you?" she asked.

"Yes," he said. He put out his hand. "I'm David Hunter." He looked at her name tag. "And you're April McKenzie."

"That's right," she said. "I'm one of the researchers here."

"What do you research?"

"Right now, I'm working on collecting the writings of Oliver Cowdery. But what can I do for you?"

"Well, I have kind of an unusual request. I inherited this piece of paper from my grandfather, and I'd like to find out more about it, if I can."

She took the paper and examined it, then handed it back.

"I know exactly what that is," she said.

"Really?"

"Yes. It's an important part of Church history." She turned to an older woman who was sorting books in a room behind the counter. "Margaret? Could you watch the desk while I help this patron?"

Margaret looked over the top of her glasses. "Of course, dear. I'm glad to see you offering such *personalized* service."

April flushed, and David looked up at the ceiling, trying not to smile.

"Come with me, please," she said.

He followed her over to the stacks, where she removed a large, black volume—*A Comprehensive History of The Church of Jesus Christ of Latter-day Saints, Volume 1.* She opened the book, then riffled through the pages, finally coming to rest at a picture of a document very much like the one David was carrying.

"That's it!" he said.

"Well, not exactly. Yours is a hand-drawn copy of the original—the one in the picture."

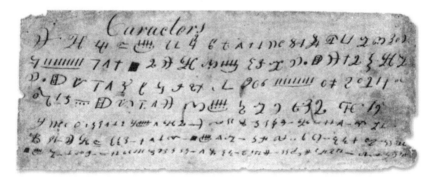

He put his document directly underneath the photo in the book, comparing the two. He could see a few differences, but they seemed to be minor.

"The Church actually has several copies of this document, all made at different times by different people. The original is owned by the Community of Christ—the Reorganized Church—in Independence, Missouri."

"Who made the original?"

"Joseph Smith. The word 'Caractors' at the top has been identified as being in his handwriting. The document is a copy of characters from the Book of Mormon—probably the one Martin Harris took to Charles Anthon."

"Wow. Can anyone read it?"

"A few people have claimed to. I'm skeptical, myself."

"If it could actually be translated, that would prove—"

She held up a finger. "It would prove the Book of Mormon is true—*if* the characters could be verified as genuine—some kind of Egyptian, for example—and they actually said something related to the Book of Mormon. But a critic would say that the characters are just gibberish—that Joseph was pulling Martin Harris's leg, or worse, defrauding him. It's even possible that Joseph was writing a message in code, seeing if anyone was smart enough to read it. He did send it to 'the learned,' after all."

David rubbed his forehead. "We never seem to get to the bottom of things, do we?"

"Oh, I don't know about that. And besides, it's awfully interesting to try."

"Do you have any idea why this one character would be circled?"

April looked again at the document—more closely this time. "No, I don't. The circle was made later, in pencil. That particular character must have meant something to someone."

"Probably my grandfather. I'd love to know what he was thinking. He was such an interesting person—quite a scholar in his own way. And this document sort of connects us; he left it to me when he died. I think he wanted to tell me about it, but then he had a stroke . . ." David paused. "Anyway, I've been hoping I'd be able to finish working out whatever it was he found."

"I see."

"If it is some kind of code," he said, "I might be able to decipher it. That's part of what I do. I work for the FBI."

"You're kidding," she said.

"No, it's true."

"I didn't know the FBI had an office in Salt Lake."

"Yup. Second East and Second South. I work on the twelfth floor."

"Not that it matters, but are you LDS?"

"Yes, but I don't go to church much. But I do come from good, solid pioneer stock. If it weren't for my dad, I'd positively ooze Mormonism every time I cut my finger."

"Your dad's not a member?"

David thought for a moment. "He's a lapsed member, I guess you might say."

April nodded. "So are there lots of Mormons who work for the FBI?"

"Are you kidding? The place is crawling with them. The FBI likes hiring Mormons. We're thrifty, brave, clean, and reverent, and we seek after these things."

April laughed. "Let's see your badge."

"Um, Eagle Scout or FBI?"

She rolled her eyes. "Okay, then. Eagle Scout."

Now a little embarrassed, David flushed, feeling his pockets. "I don't seem to have that one with me."

"FBI, then."

He reached into his coat pocket and pulled out the golden shield. "Federal Bureau of Investigation," it read. "Department of Justice."

"I've never seen a real one," she said. "Only on TV."

"Well, if you're ever in trouble, now you know who to call." He handed her his card.

"Thanks," she said. "I'll remember that."

"So what's next?"

"Would you like to look at the translations other people have come up with?"

"That would be perfect. And then I could try to identify the characters. But I'd better come back tomorrow. I have bad guys to catch, you know."

"I'll look forward to seeing you," she said with a smile.

And once again David felt the warmth spreading through his body.

HARMONY, PENNSYLVANIA, MARCH–APRIL, 1829

⊰ ≋ ⊹

I'm sorry, but I can't show you the plates, Mr. Hale. The angel commanded me that I must show them to no one." Joseph felt sorry at this turn of events, but he'd learned through hard experience the importance of obeying the Lord.

"I'll have nothing in my house that I can't see, young man. If you are unwilling, you must find another place."

"What about Emma? She's your daughter; will you turn her out as well?"

"She has cast her lot with her husband."

∧∧∧

That night, Joseph turned to his unfailing source of help. "Dear God," he prayed, "we are reduced in property, and my wife's father is about to turn us out of doors, and we have not where to go." But as he paused, the word of the Lord came into his mind: "Stop, and stand still until I command thee, and I will provide means whereby thou mayest accomplish the thing which I have commanded thee."

Joseph knew the Voice; suddenly he felt at peace. He would wait for the arm of the Lord to be revealed.

/\/\/\

In the first part of April, Oliver and Samuel left for Harmony to visit Joseph Smith Jr. The weather was cold and wet, and traveling in the mud was miserable, but Oliver was determined to meet and speak with the young Prophet.

On April 5, after days of slogging through the rain, the travelers reached Harmony, where Joseph and Emma had purchased a home and land from Emma's brother Jesse near the Susquehanna River. The two men had been walking all day, and finally, in the light of the setting sun, they approached their destination. Joseph, who'd seen them coming, came out of the house to welcome them, embracing his brother—and then embracing Oliver, much to the young man's surprise.

"I knew you were coming," Joseph said. "The Lord promised he would send means to accomplish the work. And now, here you are."

"You know I've come to help?"

"Yes. I've seen your meditations, and you know the truth, for you have seen me—and the plates—in vision."

"I've told no one of that."

"Then that is a witness to you, is it not?"

Oliver didn't know what to say. On this day, for the first time in his life, his natural eyes had beheld a prophet of God. He was tired, wet, and chilled to the bone, but his heart was full of joy.

CHAPTER 6

David felt sick. He'd spent the past hour at the Church Historical Library looking through reel after reel of microfilmed documents, and the whirling images had made him so dizzy his head hurt. He stopped spinning the handle and rubbed his eyes, then looked back at the image projected on the bottom of the machine. Didn't they ever clean the lenses on these things? The image was already grainy, but the dusty machine also projected spots and specks and even someone's thumbprint, making the document still harder to see. He used his own thumb to wipe off the lens, hoping it would make a difference. And it did—it made it worse. He rubbed his eyes again.

He was looking for "translations" of the characters from the Book of Mormon and had already found a few. April had helped him locate the possible microfilms in the library's computerized card catalog, but then she'd had to attend to other work. He wondered if her supervisor had said something to her about being so attentive to one particular patron. The thought made him smile.

The document he was looking at was a translation of the transcript characters by a professor named Barry Fell. The professor was using a different version of the transcript—one that had turned out to be a forgery. It was, in fact, the infamous forger Mark Hofmann's first important "discovery." At first David was ready to reject the possibility that the document could actually be translated, but then he realized that most of the characters were the same as the ones on the original transcript; Hofmann had simply rearranged them into vertical columns. So the professor's translation might still be valid, and it looked convincing enough. Fell had redrawn the original characters in a script he called "Maghrib," under which he'd supplied another script labeled "Modern Arabic." This David could actually read, thanks to his FBI training in the wake of 9/11, and Fell had gotten it right. "Revelation of Nefi," Fell had translated. "I have written these things. I, Nefi, a son born to sagacious parents." Maybe this was it!

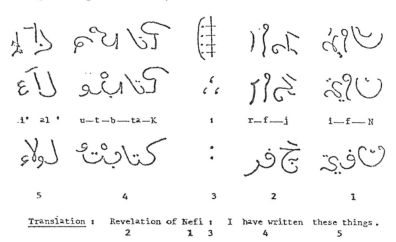

Then David cranked the film forward a few more pages, where he read a letter from a BYU professor who made a shrewd observation: Joseph Smith had drawn the Caractors transcript when he was *beginning* the Book of Mormon translation, which had nothing to do with Nephi. According to the BYU professor, the book of 1 Nephi probably wasn't translated until near the *end* of the process. So what did this say about Professor Fell's translation?

Could the BYU professor be right? David had always assumed 1 Nephi had been translated first. Well, not first, really. Everyone knew the story of how Martin Harris had pressured Joseph Smith to let him show the first 116 manuscript pages to his relatives—and then lost them. And how Joseph then found the records on the Small Plates to replace them—a story David's father had always ridiculed as being far too convenient. But at any rate, assuming there really were plates to be translated, the 116 pages would have been finished first.

David pulled a piece of paper out of his notebook and made a quick sketch; he always thought better on paper than in his head.

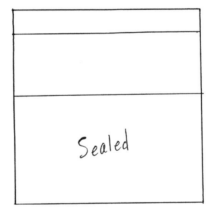

He was about to write "116 pages" in the first block, but the book had a name, didn't it? He picked up a photocopy April had given him of the preface to the 1830 Book of Mormon: "I translated, by the gift and power of God, and caused to be written, one hundred and sixteen pages," the Prophet had written, "the which I took from the Book of Lehi."

Right, David thought. *The Book of Lehi.* He penciled the name into his diagram:

And what came next? Surely someone had already been over this ground. David went out to the book stacks—with which he was now becoming quite familiar—and found the *Encyclopedia of Mormonism*. The article about the gold plates featured a diagram much like his own, but he could see immediately that the diagram was wrong—it had the plates starting with 1 Nephi. Nearby, on another shelf, he found *Story of the Formation of the Book of Mormon Plates,* which featured a similar diagram on the cover—also wrong. David gritted his teeth in frustration. Couldn't anybody get this right?

He didn't have time to work all of this out, but one thing seemed certain: 1 Nephi couldn't have come first. And that meant Professor Fell must be wrong—probably influenced in his translation by his previous cursory acquaintance with the Book of Mormon.

Earlier, David had also looked at a book called *Translating the Anthon Transcript,* which was intriguing but, he now realized, had a similar problem. The authors had identified the characters as a passage from the book of Ether, but that book was definitely translated toward the end, not the beginning. So that couldn't be right either, because these characters had been copied at the *beginning* of the translation process.

David went back to the research room, where he gathered

up his things, rewound the final tape, and switched off the microfilm machine. He felt dizzy and exhausted. And all of the existing "translations" looked like dead ends. But there was one bright spot—one that would have left his father dismayed: he sure was learning a lot about the Book of Mormon.

CHAPTER 7

᚜ ≋ ᚺ ⊐

Thornton Price sat at a sorting table in a document-storage room on an upper floor of the Church Historical Library. The room was kept at a carefully controlled temperature and humidity—a little too cool for comfort—and its rows of shelves were filled with box after box custom-made of gray, acid-free cardboard. Each box contained a document—or several documents—all of which were valuable, and a few of which were priceless. Thornton knew them well—the issues of *The Reflector* newspaper in which excerpts from the Book of Mormon were first published—illegally—by Abner Cole; the copy of the Book of Mormon Hyrum Smith was reading in Carthage Jail the day he was murdered; and even an ordinary blue paperback edition of the Book of Mormon, made not so ordinary by notations in the margins and a single signature inside the cover—"E. Presley." *Even the King needed religion,* Thornton mused.

Humming "Love Me Tender," he put on the white cotton gloves that all of the archivists wore before handling original documents. Then he picked up a bundle from a recent acquisition in Ohio—old land deeds and letters from Kirtland. Nothing very exciting, but maybe some of them would be useful. He was thumbing through them, one at a time, when he spotted a document whose handwriting he recognized. Could this be right? The paper was in bad shape, tattered and stained, especially at the bottom. But it was still readable—barely. He felt excitement welling up in his chest.

Dear Brother:

    It is with sensations of regret that I write these few lines in relation to the Book of Mormon. I cannot any longer forbear throwing off the mask, and letting you know the secret.

Following that were several lines of odd symbols, of which Thornton could make no sense at all.

Then the letter went on:

    I omit other important things which could I see you I could make you acquainted with.

Farewell untill I return,

Joseph Smith Jr.

Good grief! Thornton thought. *Set me up and then let me down.* What could the symbols possibly mean? Whatever it was, it must be something sensational. "Throwing off the mask"? "Letting you know the secret"? What did he have here?

And then he knew: He had the answer to all his problems.

Dear Brother:

It is with Sensations of regret that I write these few lines in relation to the Book of Mormon I cannot any longer forbear throwing off the mask and letting you know the secret

I omit other important things which could I see you I could make you aquainted with

Farewell untill I return

Joseph Smith Jr

CHAPTER 8

T oday work at the library was slow, so April had time to help David with his research. Since none of the "translations" of his grandfather's transcript had worked out, they were comparing the characters with Egyptian hieroglyphics, hoping to verify their authenticity that way, and were actually getting quite excited.

"Look, here's another one," April said. She was pointing at an extremely odd character in a copy of *Egyptian Grammar*, by A. H. Gardiner. To David's surprise, it matched perfectly with a character from the first line of the transcript. They had now matched nearly thirty of the transcript characters with hieroglyphs from the Egyptian dictionary—many more than they had anticipated—and not just *simple* characters, either. Many of the symbols were unusual and complex.

April read from the massive book: "This character, resembling a cursive capital 'H,' is the ancient sign of the scribe, having the meanings 'writing,' 'write,' 'polished tablet for writing,' 'made bright by scouring,' etc."

"Well, that certainly fits," David said. "How could Joseph Smith have known about all this?"

"He *didn't* know about it, and he certainly didn't make it up. These are actual Egyptian characters."

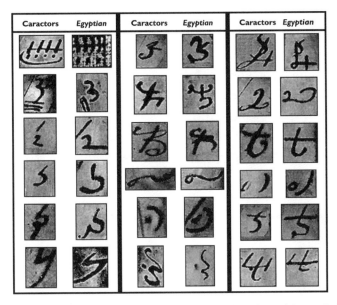

Caractors	Egyptian	Caractors	Egyptian	Caractors	Egyptian

"It sure looks that way," David said. Then his training kicked in. "You know what we need? We need a control."

"A control?"

"Yes—a known system. We need to compare the transcript with other sets of unusual characters. That will tell us whether we're on to something here, or whether this is all just coincidence."

"You mean the transcript characters might match other writing systems too?"

"Right. This is a big book, with hundreds of hieroglyphics. It would actually be surprising if some of the characters *didn't* match."

April's shoulders slumped. "I see what you mean."

"So what have we got?"

April turned to her computer. "Let's find out." David watched as she furrowed her brow, concentrating on the results that were turning up on the screen.

"Here we go," she said. "Here's the Pitman shorthand used by George Watt to record the talks in the *Journal of*

Discourses. And here's a different kind of shorthand that was used by Irish monks—it doesn't get much more obscure than that. Then we have some Phoenician characters. And here's something really unusual." She turned the screen around so he could see. "The Micmac Indian language."

"Wow, that's interesting."

Together, they pored over the strange symbols.

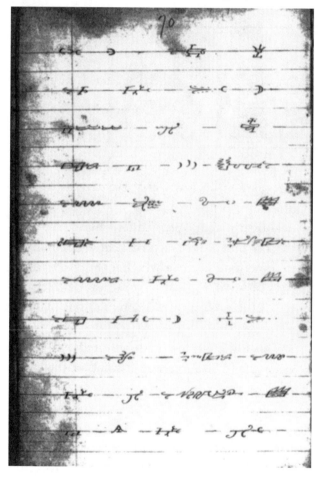

"Oh, oh," David said. "Here's a match."

"Here's another one," April replied.

During the next twenty minutes, they found several

additional matches in three of the character sets—the Micmac symbols, the archaic shorthand, and even the Phoenician script. Of particular interest was the odd black square on the Caractors transcript, which showed up in two places—in the shorthand symbols and in the Egyptian hieroglyphics they had been looking at earlier.

"So now what?" April said.

David threw up his hands. "Who knows? We're not going to prove anything working like this."

April thought for a moment. "Maybe that's the point. Maybe we're not supposed to *prove* anything. Maybe, in the end, God wants us to rely on faith."

"Maybe," David said. "But isn't faith supposed to lead to knowledge?"

/\/\/\

As David walked back to his office, he decided to take a quick detour through Temple Square. It was a little out of his way, but that was all right—it would give him a chance to enjoy the trees and spring flowers and, most of all, to think.

As he walked along the broad walkway, he looked up at the temple, noticing the symbols sculpted into the main tower. There were the clasped hands, a token of fellowship, which David had always loved. Above them was the all-seeing eye, symbolizing God's watchful care over his creations. And then, farther up on the central tower, David made out something he'd never noticed before—seven small stars carved in relief on the gray granite blocks of the temple. Together, they formed a representation of the Big Dipper. At first David was puzzled—why put the Big Dipper on a tower of the temple? And then he realized: because it points the way to the North Star—the unmoving marker that guides our way home.

David sat on the edge of one of the raised flowerbeds and contemplated the stone constellation. To astronomers, it was known as Ursa Major, the Big Bear, so called because, to the ancient Romans, it resembled that animal. But wasn't that just an accident of the earth's location? From some other planet, some other system, those stars would take on a completely different configuration. They wouldn't be the Big Dipper at all. And the North Star wouldn't be the North Star.

So it is with all the patterns of our lives, David thought. *We read into them the things we need to see.* But he couldn't help but wonder if his grandfather's transcription might yet prove to be an exception.

JULY, 1835

⊰ ≈ ⊹

Dear Brother [William W. Phelps]:

. . . You have, no doubt, as well as myself, frequently heard those who do not pretend to an "experimental" belief in the Lord Jesus, say, with those who do, that (to use a familiar phrase) "any tune can be played upon the Bible." What is here meant to be conveyed, I suppose, is that proof can be adduced from that volume to support as many different systems as men please to choose: one saying this is the way, and the other, this is the way, while the third says that it is all false, and that he can "play this tune upon it." If this is so, alas for our condition: admit this to be the case, and either wicked and designing men have taken from it those plain and easy items, or it never came from Deity, if that Being is perfect and consistent in his ways. . . .

Oliver Cowdery

CHAPTER 9

꒦꒦꒦

As the months passed, Thornton sold several historical documents to the bookstore, and life was good. His wife, Tamara, was happier—and more amorous—than she'd ever been, and Sonny and Seth, the bookstore owners, were ecstatic—they'd made a lot of money reselling those documents, with customers clamoring for more.

This one, though, Thornton was confident, would make their heads spin. He wondered how much they'd be willing to pay—surely the thing was worth a fortune.

As he entered the bookstore, Seth and Sonny looked up and smiled, then came over to greet him. They seemed especially enthusiastic today—something Thornton found a little strange.

"Hello, old buddy," Seth was saying. "It's great to see you—just great." He shook Thornton's hand, his black ponytail bobbing up and down.

"Hey, friend," Sonny said. "Do you have a new document, or are you skipping that step and just bringing us piles of cash?" His big stomach shook with laughter.

"Oh, it's a document," Thornton said. "A real doozy." He reached into his coat and brought out a single gray folder, pausing dramatically.

"Come on, come on," Sonny said. "Let's have a look."

"Not so fast," Thornton replied. "This time, it's just a copy. You'll see why."

Opening the folder, he revealed the dark, nearly illegible photocopy, which Sonny immediately snatched up. "Dear Brother," he read haltingly. "It is with sensations of regret that I write these few lines in relation to the Book of Mormon. I cannot any longer forbear throwing off the mask, and letting you know the secret."

Sonny felt around behind him. "I need to sit down," he said. Finding a chair, he lowered his enormous bulk onto the seat.

"This is an important document," Thornton said. "It's going to show that Joseph Smith was *not* what he claimed to be."

"I can't believe it. I just can't believe it," Seth said.

"You'd better believe it. The real question is, do you want to buy it?"

"Of course we want to buy it," Seth said. "You can't give this to anyone else. We'll definitely make this worth your while."

"Good," Thornton said. "We've just moved up into the big leagues. I want a hundred thousand dollars."

Seth grimaced. "We'd need to see the actual document first. I'm sure you understand."

"Sure. You bring the money and I'll bring the document. We'll meet in some public place—just like in the movies."

Sonny laughed.

"I'm serious," Thornton said.

"Okay," Seth said. "But first, Sonny and I need to talk for a minute in the back room—just a moment of privacy."

"No problem," Thornton said.

The two brothers took the photocopy and disappeared behind the counter, while Thornton scanned the stacks of books that were sitting on a display table. Finally, the brothers reappeared, all smiles.

"I'm sure we can work everything out," Seth said. "But first, we have another matter we need to discuss with you."

"What's that?"

"It has come to our attention," Seth said, clearing his throat, "that at least one of the documents you've sold us is not a newly discovered document."

"What do you mean?"

"It's a document already known to scholars."

"What are you talking about?"

"In other words, it's a document owned by the Church."

Thornton's face went white.

"So we now know," Seth went on, "that there is no stash of documents owned by some great-aunt of yours or whatever. You've been getting these documents somewhere else, haven't you, Thornton."

Thornton stared at Seth. "It was a mistake," he said. "A mistake. And this new document—the Church doesn't know about it. It just came in."

"So you stole it too."

Thornton nodded.

"Then it wasn't a mistake. You knew exactly what you were doing. So here's the deal. We're not going to buy this document—you're going to give it to us. And we're not going to sell it. Instead, you're going to help us offer it to the Church—for a very large sum of money. And if the Church isn't interested, we'll release it to the media. I'm sure they'll be *very* interested."

"What about the coded part? Maybe it's not as sensational as you think."

"Then why is it in code? At any rate, we have a friend who can work it out. I'm sure he'll be happy to be part of the deal—and so will you, Thornton, when you get your share of the money."

"You're talking about blackmailing the Church?" Thornton felt as if the floor had fallen out from under him.

"Blackmail. It's such an ugly word. Don't you think so, Sonny?"

Sonny didn't reply. He just laughed and laughed, his big stomach shaking.

CHAPTER 10

S itting at a research table in a far corner of the Church Historical Library, David and April had reached a dead end. In spite of all their work, they were really no closer to deciphering the transcript of Book of Mormon characters than they had been at the beginning. "The Moroni Code," they had taken to calling it—a joking reference to Dan Brown's bestselling novel *The Da Vinci Code* and a nod to David's FBI work. But David hadn't been able to figure it out. None of the alleged translations seemed right, and there was no way to know for sure what the characters even were. David was ready to call it quits, but he was trying to look on the bright side.

"Well," he said, "all of this has really been interesting—I have to say that. I've certainly learned a lot. And it's been really nice getting to know you, April."

She smiled, lowering her eyes, then looked back up. "You know," she said, "there is one avenue we haven't tried yet."

"What's that?"

"Come with me," she said. They stood up, and April pulled David through the library, past the front desk, and out the glass doors that led to the security guard. But instead of turning left past the guard, she went straight ahead—to a bank of elevators on the opposite wall, where she pressed the "UP" button.

"Where are we going?" David asked.

"You'll see," she said, stepping onto the elevator. "I want to show you something."

As the elevator doors opened, David was amazed. He'd never been to this part of the library before. The room was similar to the one downstairs, but there seemed to be more patrons—or employees, maybe—and they all looked very serious about what they were doing—examining microfilmed documents, looking through books, taking notes. The main room was surrounded by glassed-in offices, and the place had a quietly humming efficiency that David found quite impressive.

April walked up to the reference desk and smiled at the handsome bald fellow behind the counter. "Hi, Bill," she said. "Could we see an original copy of *The Evening and the Morning Star?*"

"Sure," Bill said. "Do you have a particular issue in mind?"

"No. Any of them would do."

"All right. I'll get you one." He put out his hand to David. "Who's your friend?"

"This is David Hunter. I've been helping him with a research project."

"Pleased to meet you, David," Bill said. "What do you think of April? She's a wonderful, um, researcher, isn't she?"

April flushed. "Bill—," she said.

"Okay, okay," he said, holding up his hands. "I'm going." He disappeared into a back room, grinning from ear to ear.

"What I'm going to show you," April said primly, "is a copy of an early Church newspaper."

"I've heard of it," David said. "Didn't it include some revelations of Joseph Smith?"

"That's part of it. Also news articles, announcements—all kinds of things."

"I don't see what that has to do with the Book of Mormon."

"Well, really, it doesn't. But just hold on a minute, okay?"

A few minutes later, Bill brought out the document. It was much bigger than David had thought it would be, and the front page featured a headline in big black letters: "THE OUT-RAGE IN JACKSON COUNTY, MISSOURI."

"Gloves," April said.

David dutifully put on the white cotton gloves, then picked up the document. Paging through it, he noticed obituaries, advertisements, letters to the editor, and much more. "I get it," he said. "It's a newspaper."

"Right," she said. "But I already told you that."

"Hmm."

"But you didn't really understand until you saw the document itself." She tilted her head. "There's no substitute for the real thing."

"So I see."

"So I think you should ask for permission to see the original transcript of the characters from the gold plates."

He looked up. "Would they let me? Would it really make a difference?"

"It might," she said. "And it wouldn't hurt to ask."

David had to fill out a form with his name, address, and phone number, and an explanation of exactly what he wanted to see and why he wanted to see it. "Just tell them about your grandfather's copy," April said. "I'm sure they'll understand."

After David was finished, Bill took the form into the back room. Finally, after a long wait, he came back. "For something like that, we'll need special permission," he said, "and we'll need to make arrangements with the Community of Christ, which owns the document. We should be able to let you know in about a week. Getting the document itself will take longer—it's in Missouri."

"That long?" David's face fell.

"Sorry we can't do any better. But that's a very important piece of history—irreplaceable."

"I understand," David said. "I'll look forward to hearing from you."

"I'll tell you what," Bill said. "We'll have April let you know."

And with that, David actually felt much better.

CHAPTER 11

⟫⟨ ≋ ⊹⟨ ⟩

It had been a little more than a week since David had asked for permission to see the original transcript of characters from the gold plates. He hadn't heard from April yet, but that morning he'd gone to the Eagle Gate building on South Temple for FBI business, then had some Chinese food at the mall, and the Church Office Building was beckoning temptingly from just across the street. *Why not?* he thought.

He crossed at the traffic light, passed the Administration Building, and walked along the beds of daffodils and tulips, passing through the now-familiar revolving door. When he went to sign in at the library security desk, the guard—one he'd never seen before—stopped him. "I'm sorry, but we're not letting anyone in today."

"What? Why not?"

"It's a security matter."

"I'm FBI, if that helps." David pulled out his badge.

"It doesn't," the guard said. "This is an internal affair."

David put his badge away. "All right," he said. "Is there any chance I could speak with April McKenzie?"

"I'll see if she's available." The guard picked up the phone and punched a button. "There's a gentleman here to see April," he said. "I see. All right." Then he hung up. "She'll be out soon. Please have a seat in the lobby."

David waited for several minutes, watching a group of people near the front door. From the men's dark suits and the women's conservative dresses, he surmised they were Church employees. They were talking excitedly and looking around the lobby. Finally, a few of them left the group and strode purposefully toward the elevators. Obviously something important was going on. Then he noticed a news crew gathering like crows outside on the plaza. They were unpacking equipment, laying down cables, and hooking up microphones and television cameras. *I'm going to be in the way here,* he thought. He was just getting up to leave when April came through the library doors. "Oh, David," she said. "I was going to call you this morning, but things have been so hectic here."

"So I gather. Are you all right?"

April smiled. "Oh, yes. But David, I have bad news. They've turned down your request to see the original transcript."

He shook his head. "I was afraid of that."

"It has nothing to do with you. We've had a security breach, and they've really got things screwed down tight."

David nodded. "So what's going on? Can you tell me?"

April sighed. "I guess so—they've already made an announcement to the press. Six of our historical documents are missing."

"Missing?"

"Stolen. At first we thought they might just have been misplaced, so we did a complete inventory. No good." She shook her head. "Those documents are gone."

David whistled. "Anything I can do to help?"

"Well, there could be. But for now, there's probably no reason the FBI would be involved."

"Right," he said. He thought for a moment. "April, listen.

After things quiet down, do you think I could ask to see the transcript again?"

"Actually," she said, "I'll resubmit your request in a couple of days. Then we'll see what happens."

"Thanks," he said. "That's great. I really appreciate it."

As David walked back to his office, he pulled out his grandfather's transcript, now as familiar as his own face. He knew every dot, every line, every squiggle. But he was beginning to doubt that he'd ever be able to solve this strangest of puzzles, this odd inheritance. *The Moroni Code,* he thought with a wry smile. And that brought his mind back to April—and to the Church Office Building. He knew that the Church—and the police—sometimes asked the FBI for assistance. If they did that now, maybe he'd be called in to help—with more important things to untangle than the faded symbols on an aging slip of paper.

He looked at his watch. It was time to go to work.

PART TWO

CHAPTER 12

⊁ ≋ ⼁ >

Several weeks had passed since David had last spoken with April, and the case of the stolen documents was being handled by the police, with no need for the FBI to get involved. So David was surprised when the Special Agent in Charge, Ted Wilcox, called him into his office on a Monday morning to talk about recent events at the Church Office Building.

"I didn't think we were involved with the stolen documents," David said.

"We're not." Now in his fifties, his brown hair tinged with gray, Wilcox was still an imposing man, with his sharp eyes— and intellect—and his bulldog chin. David had seen him in action—his skill with a gun bordered on the miraculous—and he had nothing but respect for this tireless patriot.

"So what's going on?"

"This is a different case entirely—the Church is being threatened with blackmail."

David whistled.

"Here's the note." Wilcox handed David a folded letter, which he quickly opened and read.

> We have in our possession a historical document that will destroy the LDS Church. A photocopy of that document is attached. On May 1 you will wire the sum of ten million

dollars to an offshore bank account, the details of which will be sent to you at midnight on April 30. If you fail to respond, we will release the document, including the translation of the coded portion, to the press. If you respond, however, we will place the document in your custody, safe from the public eye.

David turned to the photocopy and began to read:

Dear Brother:

It is with sensations of regret that I write these few lines in relation to the Book of Mormon. I cannot any longer forbear throwing off the mask, and letting you know the secret.

He scanned the coded section and then went on.

I omit other important things which could I see you I could make you acquainted with.

Farewell untill I return,

Joseph Smith Jr.

"That does sound incriminating," David said. "But if the coded part is so bad, why didn't they just send the translation?"

"I'll tell you what I think," Wilcox said. "They don't *have* the translation. They're just blowing smoke."

"Could be." David thought for a moment. "Or maybe they just want to make the Church squirm. Or, more likely, they don't want to give the Church a chance to preempt them or prepare damage control."

"Any of those scenarios might be right," Wilcox said. "It's also possible that the document is a complete forgery. We won't know for sure until we examine the original—although the Church's experts say the handwriting matches Joseph Smith's, and the type of code in the document was definitely used by some of the early Church leaders. You recognize it, of course."

"Masonic cipher—pigpen code. Which is trivially easy to decode. So why do they need us?"

"Because in this case, it's not trivially easy." Wilcox frowned. "Something else is going on, and the Church has asked for our assistance. That's where you come in, David. We need you to figure this out."

"Of course. I'm happy to help."

"Good. You *must* finish the decoding before May 1 so the Church will know better how to respond."

David groaned. "That's Friday."

"Then you'd better get going, hadn't you."

"Yes, sir," David said.

"Also, the Church would like you to work in their offices, where you'll have access to other historical documents that might offer additional clues."

"That would be fine." David said. He thought of April.

"When you get there, you'll need to check in with Security. But your main contact will be an employee in the Historical Library named, let's see . . ." Wilcox shuffled through his papers. "His name is Thornton Price."

CHAPTER 13

A t the Church Office Building, David checked in with the security staff. They were especially interested in knowing how many weapons he carried while on duty. The answer was two—his .40-caliber service pistol, which he kept in a holster under his suit coat, and a small .32-caliber backup pistol, which he kept strapped to his ankle.

After he'd been cleared, he took the elevator to the second floor of the Historical Department—the same floor where April had shown him the copy of *The Evening and the Morning Star.* He was met there by a Church employee who was meticulously dressed in a gray suit and maroon tie. *Expensive shoes, too,* David thought, noticing the man's gray-leather wingtips. Weren't Church employees supposed to be underpaid?

"I'm Thornton Price," the man said, extending his hand.

"David Hunter."

"Thanks for coming to help us."

"My pleasure. What's the first order of business?"

"I'll be helping you locate any documents or historical information you might need, but first our director would like to speak with you in his office. Please follow me."

Thornton led David through a long hallway, stopping at a

secretary's desk. "Go right in," she said. "Brother Nielsen is ready to see you."

Alexander Nielsen welcomed the two men into his office, where, to David's surprise, April was already sitting, looking radiant in a blue dress.

"Thank you for coming," Brother Nielsen said. "Please sit down." Tall and slender, with thinning gray hair and horn-rimmed glasses, he looked more like a college professor than the director of a Church department. David immediately liked the man.

"I believe you already know April?"

"Yes," David said. "It's great to see you again, April."

"April has told us about your grandfather's transcript of the Book of Mormon characters, and some time ago you put in a request to see the original. Isn't that so?"

"Yes," David said.

"We've made arrangements to honor that request." He opened his desk and brought out a gray folder.

"Really?" David said. "You have it?"

Brother Nielsen opened the folder, revealing the yellowed slip of paper with its rows of strange characters.

"May I look at it?"

"That's why it's here." Brother Nielsen got out a pair of white gloves, which David put on. Then David gingerly picked up the transcript. It looked quite ordinary, yet it seemed to glow with an inner beauty, and he scanned it carefully, turning the document over and over, looking for any hint that might tell him something he didn't already know.

"This document," Brother Nielsen said, "was made by Joseph Smith early in 1828, before he actually started translating the Book of Mormon." He picked up a Triple Combination. "Here's what Joseph's history in the Pearl of Great Price says about it."

The persecution became so intolerable that I was under the necessity of leaving Manchester, and going with my wife to Susquehanna county, in the State of Pennsylvania. While preparing to start—being very poor, and the persecution so heavy upon us that there was no probability that we would ever be otherwise—in the midst of our afflictions we found a friend in a gentleman by the name of Martin Harris, who came to us and gave me fifty dollars to assist us on our journey. Mr. Harris was a resident of Palmyra township, Wayne county, in the State of New York, and a farmer of respectability.

By this timely aid was I enabled to reach the place of my destination in Pennsylvania; and immediately after my arrival there I commenced copying the characters off the plates. I copied a considerable number of them, and by means of the Urim and Thummim I translated some of them, which I did between the time I arrived at the house of my wife's father, in the month of December, and the February following.

Brother Nielsen paused. "We believe the document you are holding is the one Joseph Smith described. If not, it's certainly a copy—or partial copy—made shortly after the original." Then he continued reading:

"'Sometime in this month of February, the aforementioned Mr. Martin Harris came to our place, got the characters which I had drawn off the plates, and started with them to the city of New York.'" Brother Nielsen looked up. "Joseph then quotes Martin's account of what happened next:

"I went to the city of New York, and presented the characters which had been translated, with the translation thereof, to Professor Charles Anthon, a gentleman celebrated for his literary attainments. Professor Anthon stated that the translation was correct, more so than any he had before seen translated from Egyptian. I then showed him those which were not yet translated, and he said that they were Egyptian, Chaldaic, Assyriac, and Arabic; and he said they were true characters. He gave me a certificate, certifying to the people of Palmyra that the translation of such of them as had been translated was also correct. I took the certificate and put it into my pocket, and was just leaving the house, when Mr. Anthon called me back, and asked me how the young man found out that there were gold plates in the place where he found them. I answered that an angel of God had revealed it unto him.

"He then said to me, 'Let me see that certificate.' I accordingly took it out of my pocket and gave it to him, when he took it and tore it to pieces, saying that there was no such thing now as ministering of angels, and that if I would bring the plates to him he would translate them. I informed him that part of the plates were sealed, and that I was forbidden to bring them. He replied, 'I cannot read a sealed book.' I left him and went to Dr. Mitchell, who sanctioned what Professor Anthon had said respecting both the characters and the translation."

Brother Nielsen looked up. "You know the story. I hope you'll forgive an old college professor his eccentricity in making you hear it again."

"Oh, that's fine," David said. "It certainly has more meaning when you're actually holding the document it's talking about."

"Well, do you see anything that might give you additional clues about what your grandfather was after?"

David shook his head. "I wish I did," he said. "So how did Joseph Smith do the translation?"

"The accounts vary. But they all agree that he used some kind of revelatory instrument—either the Urim and Thummim or a seer stone."

"And how did that work?"

"We don't really know." He reached for another book. "But David Whitmer, one of the Three Witnesses, recorded his view of the process. Here's what he said nearly sixty years after the publication of the Book of Mormon: 'Joseph Smith would put the seer stone into a hat, and put his face in the hat, drawing it closely around his face to exclude the light; and in the darkness the spiritual light would shine. A piece of something resembling parchment would appear, and on that appeared the writing. One character at a time would appear, and under it was the interpretation in English. Brother Joseph would read off the English to Oliver Cowdery, who was his principal scribe, and when it was written down and repeated to Brother Joseph to see if it was correct, then it would disappear, and another character with the interpretation would appear. Thus the Book of Mormon was translated by the gift and power of God, and not by any power of man.'"

David shook his head. "That seems so odd. Why was that even necessary? Couldn't he just translate through pure revelation?"

"Good question—one I thought you might ask." He turned over a few pages. "Orson Pratt, an apostle, wondered the same thing, so he asked the Prophet. Joseph told him that he needed the Urim and Thummim 'when he was inexperienced in the spirit of inspiration.' But later, 'he understood the operation of that spirit and did not need the assistance of the instrument.'"

"So by learning to use the 'spirit of inspiration,' someone might be able to figure this out?"

"Well, I believe so—God willing." Brother Nielsen put his hand on David's shoulder. "Don't give up. If this is really important to you, you'll find a way. 'Ask, and it shall be given you; seek, and ye shall find; knock, and it shall be opened unto you.' My faith is just that simple."

David nodded. But he didn't feel nearly so sure.

"But back to the business at hand." Brother Nielsen took on a more businesslike tone. "It's got to be obvious to you that the Church is rather concerned about this latest attempt to discredit us. We'll be grateful for any help you can provide. Brother Price here will be your contact, but if there is anything I can do, just let me know."

HARMONY, PENNSYLVANIA, APRIL 6–7, 1829

⋛̸ ≋ ⊣⅃

The day after Oliver's arrival in Harmony, he helped Joseph take care of some farm work, getting it out of the way so they could begin working on the translation from the gold plates. The day after that, April 7, sitting at a handmade table in the main room of the small house, the two men began working in earnest. Joseph put on the breastplate, fastening it with the metal straps around his neck and his waist. Then he fastened the Urim and Thummim to the breastplate, adjusting them like spectacles so they sat before his eyes, leaving his hands free to work. Oliver could see that the frames were made of silver, in the shape of a bow, like an 8 turned sideways—the sign for infinity. Each side of the bow held a transparent crystal in the form of a triangle, one pointing up and the other down. If they were fit together, they would have formed a Star of David. Finally, Joseph removed the cloth that was covering the plates, and for the first time Oliver saw the ancient book.

The record was composed of several hundred individual plates, the whole having the appearance of gold, and the plates were held together by three rings, in the shape of a D, running through holes at the edge. Oliver could clearly see the engravings, which were small and beautifully made. The bottom two-thirds of the stack of plates were sealed with a gold band. Joseph had already translated about a dozen of the top third—which translation, he explained, had been lost by Martin Harris. These pages were now turned over face down on the table to the right, with the remaining plates to be translated on the left—exactly the opposite of a book written in English.

Joseph had already worked out the translations for many of the characters, and the "interpreters" helped with those he couldn't manage. Now he began reading, and as he did so, Oliver began to write, using a goose quill cut with his penknife. Working clear to the edges so as not to waste the precious paper, he inscribed the words on a small "booklet" of six sheets that he had lined, folded, and sewn together earlier that morning. "And now," the Prophet dictated, "there was no more contention in all the land of Zarahemla among all the people which belonged to King Benjamin . . ."

The great and marvelous work had begun.

CHAPTER 14

⳽ ≈ ⳾

I t was 2:29 on Tuesday afternoon. David sat at a long table in a research room on the upper floor of the Church Historical Department. Thornton Price, his contact, was working nearby in case David needed anything. They'd visited briefly the day before in Thornton's office, where David noticed something he found a little odd—Thornton's desk was completely bare, except for a computer and a manila folder, marked "Current." And when Thornton had opened the top desk drawer to make a note, David had noticed that every pencil, every paper, every paper clip, practically, was meticulously stored and arranged in a white plastic tray. The man was organized, David had to give him that. But *that* organized? To David, it seemed a little compulsive, and he wondered about the fear of chaos, the urgency of control, that must motivate such a need for perfection.

David's methods were messier, usually involving papers and books stacked all over the place, with rubber bands and ballpoint pens scattered helter-skelter across the desktop. And his computer folders—they were an embarrassment to think about. Some people probably wouldn't be able to function surrounded by such clutter, but David saw it as a source of creativity, a well of ideas, and for him, it worked. Already the table where he was laboring held books, papers, and a package of yellow legal pads, and he was starting to feel right at home.

He was working on his analysis of Joseph Smith's coded letter, using a key to the symbols of the Masonic cipher—so called because it was often used by Freemasons. But David had to smile at all the lines and boxes. No wonder it was also called pigpen code.

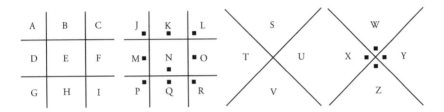

Using this simple key, deciphering the code should have been easy. But, just as Agent Wilcox had said, the symbols on the photocopy weren't cooperating. David looked at them again.

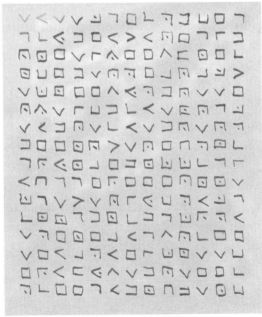

Decoded with the key, the message read like this:

```
sussjgecpdbeg
gcydeutuqegid
qnesizeevfnec
nbedsqpeaqajt
skneevypdqsse
qzsibdcusoqgj
sudqscuvdqsqp
deenqtsqehpnc
grynaednkkcgi
uhggereeeqnns
kgstsqiybpujg
cnngdncdgkrpu
speneaugvqcee
seuapueiknssb
erufyvsdqseec
pceegudnhdsnb
```

That obviously wasn't right. And that meant stronger measures were needed. He was just about to begin when April put her head around the corner of the doorway.

"Ready for a break?" she asked.

"Oh, hi, April. Well, not just yet. I've got to get this figured out."

"How's it going?"

"It's not. Here's what the code says, based on the pigpen system." He showed her the garbled "translation."

"Pigpen?"

"It's a code that was actually used quite often during Joseph Smith's day." He showed her the key. "I tried using this to decode the message, but the result is meaningless. So I thought I'd try checking character frequency."

"What's that?"

"In the English language, certain letters are used far more

often than others. For example, the letter E is the most common of all. Do you ever watch *Wheel of Fortune?*"

April smiled. "One of my guilty pleasures."

"Me too!" David said, feigning amazement. "Have you noticed that, on the final puzzle, they automatically show the letters RSTLNE? That's because those are some of the most commonly used letters—the ones any knowledgeable contestant would choose first anyway."

"Right." April nodded.

"Well, the same principle can be used in breaking a code. You count up the number of times each character is used. The one that shows up most often probably stands for E. Then T is the next most common. So if you see three characters with the most common one last and the next most common one first, the word is probably 'the.'"

"Huh?"

"Here, I'll show you. Help me count the letters."

Together, they came up with the following list:

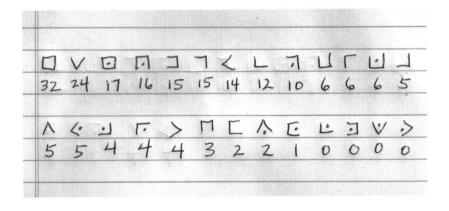

"Now, see," he said, "the square character shows up thirty-two times, more than any other, which makes sense, because in pigpen code it stands for . . . what?"

"Gosh, could it be E?" She blinked rapidly, teasing him.

"Sorry," he said. "Got into 'teacher' mode there."

"It's okay. I'm just ribbing you a little."

"And E is right. But see, that actually *doesn't* make sense. The next most frequent character should be T, but it only shows up four times two characters to the left of what should be E, with a different character between the two every time. So *one* of those combinations could be 'the,' but the others couldn't. There's only one 'the' in this message? That's possible, I guess. But not likely." He rubbed his eyes. "Well, so much for that theory."

"Sorry."

"Not to worry. Unless Joseph Smith was unusually sophisticated, it's just a matter of trying other combinations. I'll get it."

"I know you will," she said. "Are you ready for that break now?"

He looked up at the clock on the wall. It was the old-fashioned round kind, with big black numbers on a white background. The minute hand and the hour hand were also black. The second hand was red. And it was ticking—and ticking—and ticking.

LATE APRIL, 1829

⊱ ≋ ⊰

Oliver Cowdery had been growing more and more restless all morning. He and Joseph were hard at work on the translation, and he was trying to pay attention to the dictation, but now he could barely keep still.

Unnoticing, the Prophet continued to dictate: "Therefore, Helaman and his brethren went forth to establish the church in all the land . . ." But now Oliver stopped writing, putting his quill down on the table.

Joseph looked up. "Is something wrong?"

Oliver didn't know what to say.

Joseph smiled. "You want to translate."

Oliver nodded. "Yes, Brother Joseph, I do. Would the Lord permit such a thing?"

Joseph looked again into the Urim and Thummim. "There is a revelation for you, Brother Oliver. Prepare to write."

Oliver took up his quill and a fresh sheet of paper, then began to record as the Prophet dictated:

> Oliver Cowdery, verily, verily, I say unto you, that assuredly as the Lord liveth, who is your God and your Redeemer, even so surely shall you receive a knowledge of whatsoever things you shall ask in faith, with an honest heart, believing that you shall receive a knowledge concerning the engravings of old records, which are ancient, which contain

those parts of my scripture of which has been spoken by the manifestation of my Spirit.

And if thou wilt inquire, thou shalt know mysteries which are great and marvelous; therefore thou shalt exercise thy gift, that thou mayest find out mysteries, that thou mayest bring many to the knowledge of the truth, yea, convince them of the error of their ways.

Yea, behold, I will tell you in your mind and in your heart, by the Holy Ghost, which shall come upon you and which shall dwell in your heart. Now, behold, this is the spirit of revelation; behold, this is the spirit by which Moses brought the children of Israel through the Red Sea on dry ground.

And, behold, I grant unto you a gift, if you desire of me, to translate, even as my servant Joseph.

Verily, verily, I say unto you, that there are records which contain much of my gospel, which have been kept back because of the wickedness of the people; and now I command you, that if you have good desires—a desire to lay up treasures for yourself in heaven—then shall you assist in bringing to light, with your gift, those parts of my scriptures which have been hidden because of iniquity.

And now, behold, I give unto you, and also unto my servant Joseph, the keys of this gift, which shall bring to light this ministry; and in the mouth of two or three witnesses shall every word be established.

CHAPTER 15

꓿ ≈ ꓩ ∏

Thornton Price glanced over at the large red numbers on the alarm clock by his bed. The time was 11:53—nearly midnight—and tomorrow was Wednesday, the day he'd agreed to turn over the coded Joseph Smith letter to Seth and Sonny. He could hardly believe he'd gotten himself into such a mess. What in the world had he been thinking?

He rolled over to look at Tamara, who was lying next to him, breathing softly, in and out. In the waning moonlight, he admired her long brown hair, her pale white skin, felt his love for her welling up into his chest until it threatened to burst. She was the only one who had ever believed in him, the only one who had ever told him he could do great things. He wanted so much to wake her, to tell her what was going on. But he knew what her reaction would be. If he had to lose her—

The thought was more than he could bear.

He'd been over the various options so many times that he was sick of thinking about them. If he turned himself in for stealing the Church's documents, Seth and Sonny would be caught, but he'd also certainly lose his job—and probably his wife, who'd always had such high hopes for him. He might even go to prison, which made him sick to think about. How could he survive in such a setting? And the letter would eventually come out anyway, damaging the Church beyond repair.

On the other hand, if he went through with the plan, his money problems would be over—although that hardly seemed to matter anymore. And, of course, he'd be able to keep his job—assuming that the Church could somehow carry on, although he couldn't think how that would really be possible. *I should just destroy that stupid letter,* he thought, groaning at his own greed and stupidity. But if he did, Seth and Sonny would immediately turn him over to the authorities because of the other documents he had fraudulently sold them. And that would be the end of everything—everything good, everything worth living for. Above all else, he had to keep his beloved Tamara; he refused to let her go. So that was that; there was no turning back.

He felt a little bad about what would happen to the Church after the release of the letter. He'd often met with General Authorities, even knew a few of them personally, and he knew they were good men. But that didn't change what the letter showed: They were deluded—by the traditions of their fathers, ironically enough. *We all were,* Thornton thought. But now he knew better.

On his mission to Texas, he'd often borne his testimony, declaring with great fervency that he knew the Church was true. But his feelings had gotten the better of him—he'd never *really* known, never had a heavenly manifestation, for example. It was all just wishful thinking—along with the need to keep up appearances with his fellow missionaries and his family. That, he now realized, had always been his problem, his overriding weakness—and look where it had brought him.

It doesn't matter, he finally thought. *All this religious stuff is nothing but nonsense. The Church is finally getting what it deserves for being so gullible all these years. If that hurts people, it's too bad. But maybe it's all for the best.* He thought of the hymn "Oh Say, What Is Truth?"—and knew he finally had the answer. On Friday, the whole world would know, for good or for ill. He'd made his decision.

Kissing Tamara lightly on the cheek, he looked out the window into the night. The moon had gone down; the light was gone. He settled into the darkness and fell asleep.

OCTOBER, 1835

Dear Brother,—

. . . You will have wondered, perhaps, that the mind of our brother should be so occupied with the thoughts of the goods of this world, at the time of arriving at Cumorah, on the morning of the 22nd of September, 1823, after having been rapt in the visions of heaven during the night, and also seeing and hearing in open day; but the mind of man is easily turned, if it is not held by the power of God through the prayer of faith, and you will remember that I have said that two invisible powers were operating upon his mind during his walk from his residence to Cumorah, and that the one urging the certainty of wealth and ease in this life, had so powerfully wrought upon him, that the great object so carefully and impressively named by the angel, had entirely gone from his recollection that only a fixed determination to obtain now urged him forward. In this, which occasioned a failure to obtain, at that time, the record, do not understand me to attach blame to our brother: he was young, and his mind easily turned from correct principles, unless he could be favored with a certain round of experience. And yet, while young, untraditionated and untaught in the systems of the world, he was in a situation to be led into the great work of God, and be qualified to perform it in due time. . . .

Oliver Cowdery

CHAPTER 16

D avid worked late into the evening Tuesday, watching the Church employees locking doors and going home one by one, until all the lights were out—except for the ones in the decoding room, which was now completely littered with books and research material. After everyone had gone, he'd taken a break to get a drink of water, eat a couple of granola bars, and watch the sun go down from a big window on the west wall. Then, a few minutes later, a security guard had come around—evidently he'd been told that David would be working through the night and he should check on him from time to time. But now David was back at it, alone, sitting in the hard wooden chair in front of the big table with his papers spread out in front of him.

Taped to the wall above the table was a quotation that April had left for him before going home, and he read it again with a grim smile:

> "O Lord, deliver us in due time from the little, narrow prison, almost as it were, total darkness, of paper, pen and ink;—and a crooked, broken, scattered and imperfect language."
>
> —Joseph Smith, *History of the Church,* 1:299

He certainly got that right, he thought. *The Prophet understood.* But then he realized that ultimately it was the Prophet who had gotten him into this situation. He shook his head. *How strange are the events that shape our lives.* Then he looked again at his "translation" of the code:

```
sussjgecpdbeg
gcydeutuqegid
qnesizeevfnec
nbedsqpeaqajt
skneevypdqsse
qzsibdcusoqgj
sudqscuvdqsqp
deenqtsqehpnc
grynaednkkcgi
uhggereeeqnns
kgstsqiybpujg
cnngdncdgkrpu
speneaugvqcee
seuapueiknssb
erufyvsdqseec
pceegudnhdsnb
```

What had the Prophet been doing? It wasn't as if pigpen code was something unusual. In his research earlier that day, he'd turned up a diary entry from Brigham Young that had used it, and it had been a cinch to decode. Surely Joseph wouldn't have been using some other version—although David knew other versions did exist. In fact, he thought suddenly, maybe Joseph was using the cipher from Royal Arch Masonry, while Brigham was using the more commonly known cipher from Blue Lodge. That could be a possibility!

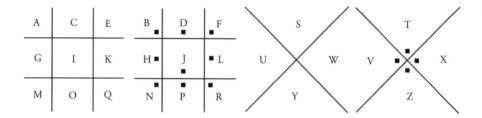

He painstakingly started translating the code, using the new key. He was only a few characters into it, however, when he could see that the result was nothing more than gibberish—an impossible combination of letters. What was he overlooking?

Could it be that Joseph had used a Caesar cipher? Now that he thought about it, it was unusual for all of the columns of letters to be exactly the same length—one of the indications that a Caesar cipher was being used. If it was, what would Joseph have used for the keyword? He tried a few different possibilities:

```
BOOKOFMORMON
sussjgecpdbeg
gcydeutuqegid
```

One character too short. How about:

```
THEANGELMORONI
sussjgecpdbeg
gcydeutuqegid
```

One character too long. Maybe:

```
JOSEPHSMITHJR
sussjgecpdbeg
gcydeutuqegid
```

Oh ho! he thought. *Just right.* But would it work? Carefully, he numbered the letters in alphabetical order, with doubled letters numbered in order of their appearance:

```
J  O  S   E  P  H  S  M   I  T  H   J  R
5  8  11  1  9  2  12  7  4  13  3  6  10
```

Then he placed the rows of letters into their numbered order, based on the order of the keyword letters:

```
sgbpsecujgsed
dugqgiucedyte
sznvqeeniceef
dqaanjebstepq
evsdsspkeenyq
idqsqguzbjsco
qcsdsqvuspduq
ntpednqeqcesh
neckggnraiydk
grneunehesgeq
tqubkjygsgsip
gnrgcpdndunck
nacvsegpeeeuq
auskssiepbuen
fveqeedrycuss
eushpnncgbedd
```

Still no good. Nothing made any sense, no matter how he looked at it. Getting up from his chair, he moved through the darkness into the restroom, where he splashed his face with cold water, then got another drink. What was he going to do?

He went back to his table, thinking hard. This kind of code was so far removed from modern cryptology, which was now based on computer algorithms and was so sophisticated as to be almost unbreakable. In fact, scientists were making advances in applied quantum theory to create a kind of coded transmission that would utterly demolish the message if anyone but the recipient even looked at it, let alone tried to decode it. Here he was, completely familiar with the latest research, and he couldn't even decipher a message in simple pigpen code from the nineteenth century.

And what about the bad guys? They'd been able to work it out, hadn't they? What made them so smart? *But maybe not,* he thought. *Maybe they don't know any more about it than I do.* On the other hand, they could have been working on this for weeks. Maybe they did know.

He stared out the window into the blackness, then looked up at the clock. It was nearly five o'clock in the morning. The sun would be rising soon. Shouldn't there be at least a glimmer of light on the horizon? But he certainly couldn't see any.

LATE APRIL, 1829

〉ᶜ ≋ ⼲

Oliver had the strangest feeling—a mixture of joy, awe, and utter terror. Wearing the breastplate and the Urim and Thummim, he was now looking at the engravings on the plates and praying for all he was worth: *Please,* he pleaded silently, *bless me to understand. Help me to translate thy word.*

Joseph had tried to explain some of the most common characters and their translation so Oliver would be better able to work out the meaning of new characters as they came up, but Oliver wasn't so interested in that; he just wanted to get down to business. Now, referring to the key Joseph had provided, he was able to make out the meaning of several of the characters—a real thrill.

At the other side of the table, Joseph was poised to write, and Oliver haltingly began to dictate: "Yea, in every . . . city . . . throughout all the land . . . which was . . . possessed . . . by the . . . people of Nephi. And it came to pass . . . that they did . . . appoint . . . priests and teachers—"

But suddenly he was overwhelmed with the magnitude of what he was doing. "Brother Joseph," he said, "I . . . I think you should translate. I may try again later, if that's all right."

81

/\/\/\

The next day, as they were translating, Joseph received another revelation for his scribe.

"Brother Oliver," he said, "the Lord has yet another revelation for you. Prepare to write."

As Joseph spoke the Lord's words, Oliver wrote them down:

> Behold, I say unto you, my son, that because you did not translate according to that which you desired of me, and did commence again to write for my servant, Joseph Smith, Jun., even so I would that ye should continue until you have finished this record, which I have entrusted unto him. And then, behold, other records have I, that I will give unto you power that you may assist to translate.
>
> Be patient, my son, for it is wisdom in me, and it is not expedient that you should translate at this present time. Behold, the work which you are called to do is to write for my servant Joseph. And, behold, it is because that you did not continue as you commenced, when you began to translate, that I have taken away this privilege from you.
>
> Do not murmur, my son, for it is wisdom in me that I have dealt with you after this manner. Behold, you have not understood; you have supposed that I would give it unto you, when you took no thought save it was to ask me. But, behold, I say unto you, that you must study it out in your mind; then you must ask me if it be right, and if it is right I will cause that your bosom shall burn within you; therefore, you shall feel that it is right. But if it be not right you shall have no such feelings, but you shall have a stupor of thought that shall cause you to forget the thing which is wrong; therefore, you cannot write that which is sacred save it be given you from me.
>
> Now, if you had known this you could have translated; nevertheless, it is not expedient that you should translate now. Behold, it was expedient when you commenced; but you

feared, and the time is past, and it is not expedient now; for, do you not behold that I have given unto my servant Joseph sufficient strength, whereby it is made up? And neither of you have I condemned.

Do this thing which I have commanded you, and you shall prosper. Be faithful, and yield to no temptation. Stand fast in the work wherewith I have called you, and a hair of your head shall not be lost, and you shall be lifted up at the last day. Amen.

CHAPTER 17

॥ᶠ ≈ ⊣ᴵ ▢

In the morning, David went for a much-needed walk around the block, then headed across the street to the food court in the mall, where he picked up a sausage-egg biscuit and orange juice at McDonald's and sat at one of the sturdy gray tables, his face in his hands and his food getting cold. He was just starting to doze off when his cell phone blared out its tinny rendition of "Hail to the Chief," which David had once programmed into it as an annoying joke, since his boss was the only one who ever called him on the thing. He kept promising himself he'd change the ring-tone to something more melodious, always right after his "next assignment."

David flipped open the phone.

"How's it going, Hunter?" Wilcox asked.

"Honestly?"

"Of course."

"Not well."

"You know, Hunter, I'm surprised. I thought you'd have this worked out in a few hours."

David rubbed his eyes. "Yeah, me too."

"Are you all right? You sound tired."

"I worked all night."

"Well, maybe it's time to pack it in."

"What?"

"It's just pigpen code. If you haven't got it by now, maybe there's nothing to get."

"What do you mean?"

"I mean it's got to be a forgery—a setup. These yahoos—whoever they are—are bluffing, hoping the Church will flinch and fork over the money. We don't even have an actual document, for Pete's sake. All we have is a photocopy. The code probably doesn't mean anything."

"Can we take that chance?"

"Oh, I don't know." Wilcox sounded frustrated.

"Look, give me today to work on it. What have we got to lose?"

Wilcox paused. "All right. But that's it. And tomorrow's Thursday anyway. The Church leaders will meet in the morning, the way they always do, and make their decision, and that will be that. I doubt they'll want to wait any longer, especially since this whole thing is so iffy. Really, they *can't* wait any longer. The deadline is Friday."

David mulled that over. "What's the worst that could happen?"

"The Church decides not to pay, the blackmailers produce a genuine document, and the translation is every bit as damaging as the rest of the letter suggests it will be."

"I can think of one thing worse," David said.

"What's that?"

"The Church decides to pay, and the blackmailers release the letter anyway."

For a long moment, the phone was silent.

"You'd better get going on that translation, Hunter."

"Yes, sir. Thank you, sir. I will."

CHAPTER 18

David worked on the letter all that morning and into the afternoon, trying every variety of pigpen code and Caesar cipher he could think of, and all with the same result: nothing. He kept raggedly poring over the columns of letters and lines of code, until, when he closed his eyes, his vision swam with broken boxes and displaced dots, and his mind felt like a computer, crunching mechanically through transpositions and combinations and probabilities. But he couldn't risk stopping; this was his last chance.

At lunchtime, Wilcox had called for a status report, insisting that David phone him as soon as he had something. But David was not optimistic. "If you don't hear from me by nine o'clock tonight," he'd told Wilcox, "consider it a no-go." April had brought him a plate of nachos and a glass of soda from the Church cafeteria, which he'd consumed with gusto while still continuing to work. At 4:30, she'd checked in again before going home for the day, this time with a turkey sandwich and a glass of chocolate milk. He'd felt a lot better after eating again, but now, at 5:30, his all-nighter was really catching up with him, and he felt a little sick from the chocolate milk. He put his head on the table, just for a brief rest—just a quick break from the relentless calculations.

/\/\/\

When David woke up, his workroom was nearly dark; some kind soul leaving for the day had even turned out the light so he could sleep—or maybe whoever flipped the switch simply hadn't noticed him dozing there behind the stacks of books and piles of paper. He looked at the clock: nearly 7:00. From the look of things, everyone had gone home. Well, not everyone. David could hear Thornton talking on the phone in the office next door—and he sounded agitated.

/\/\/\

"We are *not* meeting there," Thornton said, looking out his office window. "It's too public. Someone might see us." He was completely sick of this whole mess. The sooner it was over, the better. And he'd had enough of being bossed around. From now on, *he* was calling the shots.

"I thought you *wanted* to meet in public." Seth's voice was hollow in the tiny earpiece of Thornton's cell phone. He sounded angry. But Thornton didn't care.

"I've changed my mind. I'd like to salvage my career, if that's still possible. So I don't want anyone seeing us together."

"You have the letter?"

"Not with me. But it's in a safe place."

"Thornton. You don't trust us. I'm so disappointed."

Thornton snorted. "You're *blackmailers,* remember?"

"And you're a thief."

"Thanks for reminding me. By the way, today I mailed a letter to three friends explaining who you are and everything that's happened—a little insurance policy in case anything should happen to me. Tomorrow I'll call those friends and ask them to return the letters unopened—assuming I'm still around. I hope you're not offended by my lack of trust."

"No, of course not."

"Actually, Seth, you don't even need me to get the document. I'll tell you where I put it; you pick it up. And then we're done."

"And what if the document isn't there?"

"Why wouldn't it be?"

"Well, it's still possible you've decided to sacrifice yourself to save the Church."

Thornton laughed bitterly. "I don't think so."

"Just to make sure, you should know we have something here that's very important to you—our own little insurance policy in case your conscience has gotten to you. Her name is Tamara." He laughed. "She certainly is a beauty, Thornton. A little feisty, though."

For a moment, Thornton thought he might throw up. Then, shaking, he choked out, "If you even put a scratch on her—"

"You give us the letter, we'll give you your wife, completely unharmed. I hope you're not offended by our lack of trust."

Thornton closed his eyes, wishing all of this would just go away.

"So actually, Thornton, you'll probably want to meet with us after all—just to make sure our exchange goes smoothly."

"All right," Thornton said. He felt utterly defeated.

"Where do we need to get together?"

"Sonny's playground," Thornton said. "Basement floor. That's where I hid the letter."

Seth laughed. "Nice to see you still have a sense of humor."

"There's a glass door on the west side. I put a piece of

cardboard into the latch earlier today. The door looks closed and locked, but all you have to do is pull it open."

"Isn't there an alarm system?"

"Already taken care of. I'll meet you inside."

"You have another way in?"

"A back stairway from the parking garage. But don't worry about it. Let's just get this over with."

"Fine. Thirty minutes, Thornton."

Thornton flipped his phone shut, stalked out of his office, and slammed the door as hard as he could. The sound was still echoing as he stomped down the hall to the stairs.

CHAPTER 19

𐎛 ≋ ┿ ⊐

David had heard only half of Thornton's conversation, but that was more than enough to know what was going on, and he lost no time in following the man down the darkening hallway. But he was careful to keep back; it would do no good for Thornton to see him. *Too bad he didn't say where they're going,* David thought. *I could have a dozen agents waiting for them.* But "Sonny's playground"? Where in the world was that?

At the end of the hall, Thornton stepped into the stairwell, leaving the spring-loaded door to close haltingly behind him. But David didn't move right in. He waited until the door was almost shut, then stuck his shoe into the opening so Thornton wouldn't hear him opening the door latch. From his few days working in the building, he knew how the stairs spiraled between levels, and he waited several seconds until Thornton had gone far enough that he wouldn't see David stepping stealthily down behind him.

The stairwell was lit at intervals by fluorescent lights shrouded with yellowing plastic panels, giving the place a stark, other-worldly appearance—a vertical universe of steel and concrete, inhabited by shadows. Farther down, David could tell, some of the lights were out, and eventually he and Thornton had to move more slowly, as if linked by an invisible chain, descending together into the darkness. At this point, David had to be especially careful—if Thornton stopped, he could easily bump into him. So he listened intently, keeping track of Thornton's scuttling steps on the stairway below, feeling his way down and around the steel banister. The stairs had to end eventually. Didn't they?

Finally, David made out a dim glow, heard a doorknob turn. Thornton must have reached the bottom. Again, David held back until the door had almost closed. But this door, David now saw, had a narrow window running up its right side, the glass reinforced with steel mesh. Through the window, he could see Thornton in an empty underground parking lot, standing next to a concrete pillar, talking on his cell phone. *I hope he didn't see me*, David thought. *And surely he didn't hear me.* He knew he'd been utterly quiet. And, to David's relief, Thornton didn't look his way. He seemed to talk casually for a few more minutes, staring off across the dimly lit parking stalls. Then he closed his cell phone and walked slowly into the shadows.

/\/\/\

"Thornton's being followed." Seth shut his cell phone with a snap.

"Oh, great."

"By the FBI guy who's been trying to decode the letter."

"Unsuccessfully, I hear." Sonny laughed.

"Don't underestimate him. We need to be very careful." Seth rubbed his face. "I hate complications."

"Can't Thornton handle him?"

Seth snorted. "Are you kidding? He doesn't have the guts."

"We always have to do *everything*."

Seth looked at his watch. "We need to get moving if we're

going to get there first." He swung open the back door of the bookstore.

"What are we going to do with her?" Sonny nodded toward Tamara, who was fastened to a chair with duct tape. The tape around her mouth kept her from talking, but her dark eyes were on fire.

Seth grinned. "I can think of a couple of things."

"You're disgusting."

"Oh, like you haven't been thinking the same thing."

"Well, maybe. But I wouldn't really do it." Sonny paused. "That would be *immoral*." Then he laughed.

Seth rolled his eyes. "Let's just get her into the van. We have a meeting we need to attend."

Near the north wall of the parking garage, David was standing behind a concrete pillar, trying not to breathe. Thornton was just twenty feet away, fiddling with the latch on a rusty iron door, and David could hear him muttering under his breath. Finally he heard a loud clank, and the door creaked open—and then creaked shut. *Not good,* David thought; he wouldn't be able to reopen the door without Thornton hearing him. Going to the door and putting his ear to the crack in the doorway, he listened as Thornton walked quickly ahead, the footsteps finally fading into silence. He forced himself to wait another full minute, counting off the seconds one by one. Then, with infinite slowness, he opened the door, gritting his teeth and stopping at each tiny squeak.

When the door was open far enough, David squeezed through the crack, leaving the door open. Then he put his hands out, feeling his way along. Concrete walls, but rough this time, not finished. And no fluorescent lights; evidently the passage wasn't often used or maintained. He thought of the tiny flashlight on his keychain, but he didn't dare use it—at least not yet. Then, as his foot caught the bottom of a rising stairway, he wished he had. He stumbled heavily and fell, catching himself with splayed-out hands. His palms burned, but the real pain was in his right knee. Reaching down, he felt his torn pant-leg, the wet, warm blood. He rose shakily to his feet, listening, waiting.

Nothing.

The darkness, the silence, were overwhelming. And for the first time in a long time, he prayed. *Please protect me,* he pleaded. *I've been too arrogant, too full of doubt. Watch over me and help me do what I need to do.*

Nothing changed. But his breathing seemed easier, his pain lighter. He took out his keys and turned on the flashlight. The bulb was dim but steady, and though he couldn't see far, he moved ahead, more cautiously this time, slowly mounting each stair, making his way up through the blackness.

APRIL, 1829

꙰ ≋ ꙰

. . . Verily, verily, I say unto thee [Oliver Cowdery], blessed art thou for what thou hast done; for thou hast inquired of me, and behold, as often as thou hast inquired thou hast received instruction of my Spirit. If it had not been so, thou wouldst not have come to the place where thou art at this time.

Behold, thou knowest that thou hast inquired of me and I did enlighten thy mind; and now I tell thee these things that thou mayest know that thou hast been enlightened by the Spirit of truth; yea, I tell thee, that thou mayest know that there is none else save God that knowest thy thoughts and the intents of thy heart. I tell thee these things as a witness unto thee—that the words or the work which thou hast been writing are true. . . .

Behold, thou art Oliver, and I have spoken unto thee because of thy desires; therefore treasure up these words in thy heart. Be faithful and diligent in keeping the commandments of God, and I will encircle thee in the arms of my love.

Behold, I am Jesus Christ, the Son of God. I am the same that came unto mine own, and mine own received me not. I am the light which shineth in darkness, and the darkness comprehendeth it not.

CHAPTER 20

᠈� ≋ ᠊ᡰᠯ ᴇ

The stairs seemed to go up forever, but finally Thornton reached the top and pulled open the door he'd jimmied earlier that day. But he didn't go in. Instead, he held his breath, listening for David, who couldn't be that far behind him. *Seth and Sonny had better already be here,* he thought. *I'm not doing their dirty work.*

He listened again, but the stairwell was silent. Where had David come from, anyway? And then he realized: He'd been there all along, hiding in the research room with the lights out. He must have suspected Thornton from the beginning. Thornton shook his head. The guy was good. Quiet, too—Thornton had never heard a thing. But he'd been up and down the history department's stairwell hundreds of times over the years, knew exactly what the upstairs door sounded like when it closed. But this time it hadn't closed; someone had been holding it open, waiting to go down. And that's when he knew he was being followed.

Thornton pulled his flashlight out of his pocket and threw the beam around the room, which was otherwise lit only by the last of the daylight coming in through the basement windows. The flashlight was a windup model—no batteries—with blue diodes for light, and it had been a lifesaver going up those back stairs. *Poor David,* he thought. *He must have had a rough time.* The thought made him smile.

Thornton walked through the door onto the bottom floor of the Pioneer Memorial Museum, run by the Daughters of the Utah Pioneers. The building was situated on a hill, up by the Capitol, and Thornton sometimes walked there during his lunch hour to browse the dusty exhibit cases, the fascinating artifacts from days gone by. One case held a folded square of paper labeled "Mnemonic Chart" in the handwriting of Wilford Woodruff, who had peppered its center with a series of strange, faded symbols. Another held a seerstone kept by old Bishop Kessler—a tiny, rounded crystal protected by a black metal sleeve. Vaguely, he wondered how the bishop had used the thing. And upstairs, Thornton knew, was a "bloodstone" charm that Brigham Young carried for protection when traveling into dangerous places—something Thornton wouldn't mind having right now.

At the museum he sometimes bumped into Sonny, who especially liked to prowl the back room where the old books and manuscripts were kept, many of them priceless. *Sonny's playground,* he thought. If Sonny went missing from the bookstore, Seth always knew where to find him. Thornton was tempted to go up to the manuscript room himself; maybe he could grab a few things. But he'd never be able to sell them; everything there was too well known. *And besides,* he reminded himself, *that's how I got into this mess.*

He looked at the broken door. *Too bad I jimmied it,* he thought. *I probably could have locked it again.* But then he couldn't have gotten in to begin with—at least not the way he'd come. He tried to block the opening with a display case, but the thing was huge—and heavy, the frame made of oak. After a futile bout of shoving, he decided Seth and Sonny would have to find a way to stop David themselves. So he began threading his way through the seemingly endless maze of rooms—the place was enormous. And with night coming on, it was unbelievably creepy. Strange shapes lurked in every corner—in one room, a mannequin in a top hat nearly gave him heart failure. Finally, he reached the door on the west side of the building. He couldn't see anyone, but maybe they were hiding in the shadows. "*Seth!*" he hissed. "*Sonny!*" But no one answered. Then he thought about Tamara, wondered if she really was all right. *She'd better be,* he thought. He hated violence. But if he had to . . . He let the pictures play in his mind, growing angrier by the minute. Then he looked at his watch, waited, peered into the darkness. David could show up any minute. Or maybe he was taking his time, looking carefully through the rooms one by one so Thornton couldn't sneak up on him. He listened again, this time more intently.

Where *were* those guys, anyway?

CHAPTER 21

꙼ ≋ ⼮

So how do we get her into the van?" Sonny asked.

"Just pick her up and put her in," Seth replied.

"I can't." Sonny paused, looking down. "I'm too fat."

"I didn't mean you had to do it alone." Seth shook his head, then put his arm around his brother's shoulders. "You need to start walking more. You really should pay more attention to your health." He went around to the side of the chair and helped Sonny lift Tamara, bound, gagged, and glaring, into the back of their old white cargo van. They used the van for transporting books, and it was the beloved subject of their benign neglect, like a dog that gets scratched, fed, and watered but never taken to the vet. It was *long* past due for an oil change, although the brothers did add a quart from time to time to keep the thing going. The cargo compartment, scented with the bloom of stale tobacco, was littered with cardboard boxes and empty beer cans, and the brothers had a bit of trouble pushing the debris out of the way so they could slide the legs of the chair between the ridges on the metal floor, the decorative feet stuttering and screeching like chalk on a chalkboard. Tamara wasn't making things any easier; she kept squirming and moaning and trying to break free.

"Maybe we should hit her over the head," Sonny suggested.

Seth looked disgusted. "We're not going to hit her over the head. Man, you've been watching too many movies."

"What if she falls over?"

"She's not going to fall over. What do you want me to do, install seatbelts and shoulder restraints?"

Sonny snickered. "I think she's restrained enough already."

"Exactly. She'll be fine—if she'll just *keep still*"—emphasizing the words for Tamara's benefit. "And besides, we've *got* to get going. We don't have time to fool around."

They got into the van. Seth stomped the accelerator and twisted the key, and the engine coughed reluctantly into life. He pulled the van into the alley behind the store, then out onto the road, where it haltingly got up to speed. Then he stepped on it. As he approached the turn onto State Street, Sonny gripped the dashboard. "Slow down! We have a passenger in back, remember?"

They made the turn, but Tamara's chair went over with a crash. Seth pulled over, and the brothers ran to the back of the van, pulled open the doors.

"I *told* you she might fall over. Now look at her."

Tamara's head had hit the tire jack. She lay awkwardly on the metal floor of the van, taped in a sitting position to the chair, her head lolling to the side. They couldn't see any blood, but she'd been knocked completely unconscious, and she was going to have a whale of a bruise above her right ear.

Seth ripped the tape from her face so she could breathe more easily. "Well, at least she'll be quiet for a while."

They moved the chair back to the center of the van but left it lying down so there'd be no more accidents. Then, in the glow of the setting sun, they headed up State Street toward the Capitol, more cautiously this time. But now, going uphill, the van wasn't running well at all. Seth kept pumping the accelerator and swearing, and Sonny was nervously wiping his face, wishing they'd hurry up and get there. And that's when the motorcycle cop pulled them over with a flash of his lights. Dismounting, he walked to the driver's-side window, which Seth cranked down with a look of concern.

"Good evening, Officer," he said.

"May I see your license and registration, please?"

Sonny pulled out his documentation, which the officer scanned with his big flashlight.

"Was I doing something wrong?"

"Not really," the officer said. "But you seem to be having problems. You need some help?"

"We'll be all right. I think we have water in our gas tank."

"Why don't you pop the hood," the officer said. "Let's take a look."

"Sure," he said. "If it's not too much trouble." He glanced over at Sonny, who was trying to blend into the upholstery.

Seth flipped the latch, then stepped out of the van and around to the front, where he raised the battered hood, gratefully hiding the windshield and the van's unusual cargo.

Using his flashlight, the officer followed the gas line from the carburetor down to a clear-plastic fuel filter. Once the paper inside had been yellow; now it was a filthy black.

"There's your trouble," the officer said. "Your gas line's clogged."

"I'll be darned," Seth said.

"You know what we can do . . ." The officer thought for a second. "Do you have a drinking straw?"

"I'll see." Seth walked over to the passenger door and tapped on the glass. Sonny rolled down the window, pale as death.

"We need a drinking straw, Sonny. Would you mind looking through the glove compartment?"

His hands shaking, Sonny opened the little door, then scrounged through the fuses, cigarette packages, and dead flashlight batteries, finally coming up with a paper-wrapped straw from McDonald's. Seth exhaled with relief, then walked back to the front of the van. "Here you go, Officer," he said.

"Thanks." The officer looked at the straw, obviously thinking about what to do, completely engrossed in his task. "Uh, would you mind holding my flashlight for a minute?"

"Not at all."

Seth held the long, heavy cylinder while the officer unwrapped the straw, then, using his pocketknife, cut off a one-inch section. "Now shine it on the fuel filter." With a couple of twists, the officer removed the filter from the gas line and replaced it with the piece of straw. "That won't last long," he said. "You should get a new filter first thing tomorrow. But it will get you up the hill."

"That's amazing," Seth said. "I can't believe how you did that."

The officer beamed with pleasure.

Then Seth clubbed him in the head with the flashlight.

Sonny burst out of the van. "Are you crazy?"

"Well, we can't have him looking in the van, now can we?"

"He wasn't going to look in the van. He was just—"

"You don't know *what* he was going to do. What if he shined his flashlight back there?" He waved his hand, then slammed the hood. "What if he followed us up the hill?"

Sonny put his face in his hands. "We're going to be in so much trouble . . ."

"We're *already* in trouble," Seth said. "And besides, now we have a gun." He grabbed the pistol from the officer's holster, weighed it heavily in his hand.

Sonny closed his eyes. "Don't kill him, Seth. Please don't kill him."

"We have to," he said. "He knows who hit him. He can identify us."

"Yeah, but then the cops will really be after us. And with your record . . ."

Seth rubbed his forehead, then swore, pointing the gun menacingly at the unconscious officer.

"Don't do it, Seth."

Seth closed his eyes, finally getting hold of himself. "Okay," he said, lowering the gun. "Okay."

"Maybe we can just tie him up," Sonny said. "We've still got plenty of duct tape."

Seth grumbled, but together they bound the man's hands and feet, put tape over his mouth, and dragged him behind some bushes in front of a nearby apartment building. Then they got back in the van, and Seth fired up the engine, which now purred contentedly. It hadn't run that smoothly in months.

CHAPTER 22

꙼꙼꙼꙼꙼

After walking up all those steps, David's knee was throbbing with pain, although the bleeding had finally stopped. His keychain flashlight had run out of power about halfway up the stairs. He'd climbed a few more steps in darkness, then remembered his cell phone, which provided a passable light the rest of the way up. At one point he'd tried to call Wilcox, but deep inside the concrete walls, he couldn't pick up a signal. Now, at the top, he couldn't call without the risk of being overheard. *I guess I won't be getting any help,* he thought, shaking his head. And besides, he had no idea where he was—all the display cases made the room look like some sort of museum. And then he realized: It *was* a museum—but certainly not the Church's historical museum near Temple Square. What was this place?

He didn't walk in right away; instead, he looked around cautiously in the dim light, noting the oval pictures lining the walls, a collection of spinning wheels, an old pump organ in the corner. Thornton could be anywhere—unless he'd heard David and run. But that seemed unlikely. And Thornton had a document to deliver—the original of the one that had given David so much trouble over the past few days. *If I can get my hands on that,* he thought, *I can end this whole thing.* He put his hand on his gun. He needed to find Thornton—before the other blackmailers showed up. *Or maybe,* he thought, his stomach sinking, *they're already here.*

∿∿

Thornton had never in his life used a needle and thread, but he was looking at a collection of antique sewing machines in the basement of the museum—in particular the third one from the left. Lifting the old wooden cover, he breathed with relief; the letter was still sitting where he'd hidden it earlier that day. He doubted that the cleaning crew would engage in a sudden frenzy of dusting sewing machines, but he supposed it was possible.

He picked up the letter that had caused him so much grief. Soon he'd give it to Seth and Sonny, and the whole business would be over—except for the money. *I wonder if I'll get my share,* he thought. The Pitt brothers weren't exactly honorable men—but then, neither was he, anymore. He didn't really care. As long as he got Tamara back in one piece, nothing else mattered. And he was holding her ransom in his hand—surely the strangest ransom the world had ever seen.

He was about to take the letter to the side door so he could give it to Seth and Sonny, but then he had another thought: Until he knew that Tamara was all right, he'd leave it right where it was. He put the letter back, then closed the old wooden lid. *It's additional leverage,* he thought. It wasn't much. But it might make the difference in whether Tamara came out of this unharmed.

What about a weapon? One display case, locked, was full of old rifles and ammunition, but he doubted that any of them still worked. And even if they did, they'd probably be as dangerous to the shooter as they were to the target. But if not a gun, then what? There were some rusty old swords in there too, but he really couldn't imagine himself swinging one of those around; the hilt would probably break off anyway. And if Seth and Sonny saw him with a sword, they'd absolutely howl with laughter. Then he spotted a barrel full of canes. One of them, dark and heavy and polished with age, looked as though it would make a fine weapon—at least for whacking someone over the head. He picked it up by the handle; it felt solid, substantial, comfortable in his hand. Someone back in the 1800s must have loved the thing. He swung it at an imaginary opponent, then felt a little foolish. But maybe it would come in handy.

If Seth and Sonny didn't get here soon, he might have to use it on David, although he hoped that wouldn't be the case. But if David got in the way . . . He smacked the cane several times into his palm. Then, his heart sinking, he remembered that David was carrying a gun. His cane would be no match against that. Would David really shoot him? It was a possibility, he had to admit—unless he could take David by surprise and clobber him before David got off a round. Was he capable of such a thing? He wasn't sure. But maybe it didn't matter, since he hadn't even seen David. Where was he? *And where were Seth and Sonny?*

David was going through the museum room by room, looking for Thornton but keeping low, winding his way around the display cases and trying to take in the whole room before crossing any open space. So far there was no sign Thornton was even there. Finally, he got to the last room, back on the left, where the last light from the sunset was coming in through a glass door. Remembering Thornton's telephone conversation, he realized that must be where the blackmailers would be coming in. *They could even be there now,* he thought.

He cautiously crawled behind an exhibit of old train tracks, which were standing upright like a rickety ladder, looking more like a picket fence than something a locomotive could run on. But the tracks did offer protection, back in the darkness, and he could look out through the battered pine cross-ties at the rest of the room without being seen. If it came down to it, he could even fire his gun from here. He hoped he wouldn't have to. But he pulled it out of its holster just in case.

He remembered playing hide-and-seek as a kid, crawling into a water culvert at the end of the block near his parents' house. It was dark and muddy and crawling with ants, but he'd stayed there, peering out through the long grass until all of the other kids had given up. Then, wet, filthy, and triumphant, he'd emerged from his hiding place—he'd won the game. He'd also learned patience and endurance—traits he had honed further over the years.

He shifted his weight, trying to get more comfortable, watching for any sign of movement near the door. But the room was utterly still, utterly quiet. And that's when "Hail to the Chief" shattered the silence—his cell phone was ringing, and he'd never heard anything so loud in his life. *Nice timing, Wilcox,* he thought, fumbling to get the thing out of his pocket and turned off. He finally got it quiet. But then he felt a sharp pain on the side of his head, and the darkness exploded into fireworks, red, white, and blue, fading into black. He slumped to the floor, unconscious.

⋀⋁⋀

Thornton looked down at David. He'd actually hit the guy—and hard, too! He was a little surprised at his own strength. But there David was, crumpled up like a paper doll, still as death, his eyes closed. *I hope I didn't kill him,* he thought. He put his hand under David's nose, felt the breath moving in and out. *He's still alive,* he thought. He was glad.

Stealing was one thing; killing was another. Then he noticed the gun. Almost against his will, he pulled it out of David's hand. It was heavier than it looked—and it looked enormous. He *really* didn't want to use that. But if he had to, it would be a lot more protection—and a lot more persuasive—than someone's old walking stick. On his way back to the door, he put Brigham Young's cane back into the barrel.

CHAPTER 23

꙰ ≋ ㆔ Ｅ

Seth and Sonny parked the van on the west side of the Pioneer Memorial Museum, close to the glass door leading into the basement. The sun had gone down, but a twilight glow still lit the sky with red and gold, the evening stillness broken only by Tamara's harangue from the back of the van. She'd awakened and had really been letting them have it. Seth was amazed; the woman knew words he hadn't heard since his stint in the state pen. They left her in the van, still taped to the chair, and with no one left to yell at, she finally quieted down. As they walked up the sidewalk and opened the door, Seth saw that Thornton was waiting for them. And to Seth's surprise, he had a gun.

‧‧‧

Holding up his weapon, Thornton tried to sound nonchalant. "Good evening, gentlemen," he said coolly.

"Got ourselves a gun, do we?" Seth said.

"Just a little insurance." Then Thornton noticed the gun sticking out of Seth's belt. "I see you came prepared." He tried to feel calm, but his heart was pounding at this terrifying development. "Why don't you just slide that on over here."

"Sorry, Thornton. I can't do that. Are you going to shoot me?"

"If I have to." His voice shook.

"No, you're not. And I'm not going to shoot you. I brought this to take care of your FBI friend. Where is he, by the way?"

Thornton thought of David lying unconscious in his hiding place behind the railroad exhibit. He imagined Seth striding over to the helpless figure, blowing a hole in his chest, then walking carelessly away. Thornton closed his eyes, willing the picture out of his mind.

"He never showed up," Thornton said.

"I thought he was following you."

"He was. He must have had an accident on the back stairs. Without a flashlight, they're a little . . . dangerous." He forced himself to laugh.

"What did you do, push him?"

"I might have helped him along a little."

Seth laughed. "You've got more guts than I thought."

"Remember that," Thornton said. "Now where's Tamara?"

"Out in the van."

"Is that the truth?"

Seth opened the door. "Ask her yourself."

"Tamara," Thornton yelled. "Are you okay?"

Her reply, slightly muffled by the walls of the van, came drifting over the lawn. "I will be when you get me out of here!"

"That's Tamara, all right." Thornton smiled in spite of himself, then frowned. "You actually tied her up?"

"Well, we couldn't let her get away."

"Real nice, Seth."

"Look, just give us the letter and we'll let her go."

"Other way around," Thornton said. "You give me the keys. I'll get in the van. Then I'll tell you where the letter is. When you've got it, I'll drive away."

"I don't think so."

Sonny broke in. "You guys are making this way too hard. Look, do it this way: Thornton keeps his gun out while we get the letter. Once we've got it, there's no reason to shoot anybody, or to keep Tamara. Right? So then we all put our guns away and get out of here. Does that sound reasonable?"

Thornton pondered the proposal. "Actually," he said, "I think it does."

"Sounds okay to me," Seth said.

"All right," Sonny said. "Where's the letter?"

"Behind you, in the sewing machines—third one from the left. It's under the wooden cover."

Thornton kept his gun trained on Seth while the brothers retrieved the document.

"We've got it," Sonny said. "Now put your gun away."

Thornton didn't move, still watching the ex-con.

"It's okay, Thornton," Seth said. He held his hands in the air. "I'm not holding a weapon."

"Keep your hands up until I put it away," Thornton said. He kept his eyes on Seth, finally slipping the weapon under his belt.

With the gun put away, everyone relaxed. The relief was palpable. Then Sonny started to laugh. "See?" he said. "Was that so hard?"

"Nice work, brother," Seth said, patting him on the back.

⋀⋁⋀

David immediately stepped out of the shadows with his backup gun drawn and ready for action. "You can put your hands back up now—all of you," he said. But to his amazement, Seth threw open the door and pounded down the sidewalk toward the van. After a split second of hesitation, Thornton dashed through doorway close behind. Sonny was struggling to run, pumping his big legs and pushing his enormous bulk out of the building. David fired a warning shot, but Sonny was already lumbering down the sidewalk, moving surprisingly fast for a man his size.

With the men outside, David moved to the side of the door, held it open a couple of inches, and peered through the crack. "Stop right there!" he yelled. "Stop, or I'll shoot!" Seth dove behind the van, then fired toward the door of the museum; the thick glass shattered, exploding into the room. Then he fired again, trying to give Sonny a chance to get to safety. David immediately leaned out of the doorway and fired back, a little erratically, putting a hole in the van's back bumper.

"Come on, Sonny!" Seth yelled. "You can make it!" The big man slipped on the grass, half falling, then scrambled to his feet. His eyes were full of terror. David felt time slow to a crawl as he watched Sonny moving inch by inch, as if in a dream. Again Seth shot at David, then again, the gun booming over and over in the evening air, the metallic smell of gunpowder moving on the breeze. But now, his arms churning, his breathing labored, Sonny veered to come around the van, and as Seth fired once more, Sonny took the bullet squarely in the chest, his ungainly body jerking backward, then sprawling awkwardly into the street. He groaned, wheezing out a froth of blood and bubbles. Then he lay still.

Seth looked stunned, bewildered. "Sonny!" he yelled. "Sonny!" Steadying his gun, he took another shot, and David felt himself thrown back through the doorway with incredible force, his shoulder burning with pain. Slumped against a display case, he put up his hand, then drew it back. It was covered with blood. He fumbled with his cell phone, tried to dial, but for some reason his hand wasn't working right, and the air seemed murky, his eyes refusing to focus. Dimly, he could hear the van roaring off into the distance. They'd gotten away.

Again he tried dialing, his hands shaking, and this time Wilcox answered. "David!" he said. "Thank heavens. Did you get the translation?"

"No," he said. "I'm sorry." He felt the room closing in, the darkness descending. The translation seemed a lifetime away.

CHAPTER 24

David tried to open his eyes, but when he did, the room spun in circles around his head—or maybe his head was spinning in circles around the room; he wasn't really sure. But he could tell that someone was kneeling near his side, pressing on his shoulder, and the pain was excruciating. Who would do such a thing? He moaned, tried to turn away, but the person held him in place, pressing, pressing. "Stop," David whispered. "You're hurting me."

"Just hold still," the person said. "You've been shot, and you're losing blood. If I stop, you could die. Try to hold on; the ambulance will be here soon."

David opened his eyes a little, took in the shadowy figure hovering over him. His head was still swimming, but his vision cleared enough to make out the person's features.

"Thornton," David said. Now he was really confused. "I thought you got away with the blackmailer."

Thornton shook his head. "I wasn't going to just let you die."

"You could have," he said. "I'm surprised you didn't."

"I'm not that bad," Thornton said. "Just stupid." He paused. "Besides, Seth took off before I could get into the van. That made the decision a lot easier." He smiled wryly.

"Where's your wife?"

"Seth's still got her, but I think he'll let her go as soon as he gets to a safe place. She'd be a nuisance to keep, and he'll be on the run."

"What if he doesn't?"

Thornton grimaced. "Don't even think that. Honestly, I'm scared to death."

"What about you? You're not going to run?"

"I'm going to turn myself in. I've made a mess out of things, but that's all ending, here and now. Maybe somehow I can put things together again." He shook his head. "Tamara will be through with me."

"Don't be so sure. Sometimes people surprise you." David managed a smile.

"I'll lose my job."

"Yeah."

"And go to jail."

"Probably. But you've helped yourself by not running— and by saving my life."

"I was wondering about that."

"They take stuff like that into consideration."

"Yeah, well, I'm also the one who clubbed you in the head. Sorry."

"*I* was wondering about *that*. Why didn't Seth kill me while I was out?"

Thornton shrugged.

"You saved me then, too, didn't you. That's twice."

"He would have shot you. I told him I pushed you down the stairs."

"You probably could have," David said. He gripped Thornton's wrist. "Thanks for letting me live." He winced at the pain. "Thanks for not leaving me here to die."

Thornton nodded. Then David was quiet. The loss of

blood was taking its effect. He closed his eyes. In the distance, he could hear sirens. Soon they got closer. Then he felt people lifting him up, putting him onto a stretcher. The pain crashed over him like a tidal wave. Once again, the world went dark.

CHAPTER 25

꙰ ≈ ꙳

Officer Carl Davis, with the Utah Highway Patrol, was cruising west on I-215. The night was beautiful, the sky clear, and the full moon was lighting up the road. But he'd had his fill of tailgaters, speeders, and drunk drivers. Now he was looking forward to going home for the night, spending time with his wife, maybe watching a little television.

As he came around a curve approaching State Route 201, his watchful eyes caught something unusual ahead of him, off in the shadows of the cottonwoods on the side of the road. It looked like a kitchen chair, but surely that couldn't be right. As he slowed down to look closer, though, he could see that it was. And on the chair was a woman, her face red, her hair in tangles, scowling as the semi trucks and automobiles whizzed past, unnoticing, in the moonlight.

He pulled carefully off the highway, then drove up slowly behind the chair, turned on his spotlight, and radioed in to headquarters. As he got out of his vehicle, he could see that the woman had been fastened to it with duct tape. Something was very wrong here.

"It's about time," the woman said. "I suppose you've been busy doing something else that was *really* important."

Ignoring her sarcasm, the officer shined his flashlight

around the area, looking for anything unusual. "What's going on here?" he said.

"It's a long story."

"I want to hear every detail. But first let's get you off of this chair." He pulled out a pocketknife and cut through the tape holding her arms and legs in place. "Are you all right?"

"I am now." She stood up awkwardly, then rubbed her wrists. "I could stand to go to the bathroom, though. And my head hurts." Gingerly, she touched the area above her right ear.

"I'll take you to the station," he said. "We'll have a medic look at you."

The two got into the patrol car, and the officer pulled back onto the highway. "So what happened?"

"I was kidnapped." the woman said. "I'm okay, but I'm worried about my husband. There was a gunfight—I was inside a van, but I could hear the shooting, and I heard him yelling."

"You're Tamara Price, aren't you."

"You know about this?"

"Heard it on the radio—which reminds me . . ." The officer radioed in. "I've got Tamara Price here. She seems all right, but we'll need someone to look at her and make sure." He signed off.

"Is my husband all right?"

"He's not hurt."

Tamara breathed with relief.

"He is in custody, though."

Tamara closed her eyes. "I can't believe he'd do anything wrong. What happened?"

"We're still trying to work that out." The officer paused. "I'm sorry you've had to go through all this."

"Thanks," Tamara said. "And thanks for getting me off that highway." Then, for the first time in all that had happened, she started to cry.

CHAPTER 26

⟫⟨ ≋ ⊬ ⌐

When David woke up, he had no idea where he was, but the sky was impossibly blue, and the flowers were enormous, blossoms of pink, red, yellow, and orange, covering the landscape for miles around. After the flowers came groves of pine and aspen, and in the distance purple mountains towered over the scene.

A gravel path stretched out in front of him, beckoning, and David followed it, walking through the fields, which eventually became acres of bluebells as high as his shoulders. The sight—and the scent—were overpowering, mingling with the sky until the whole world burned with blue. He walked for hours, the only sound the buzzing of bees among the flowers and the crunch of his feet on the gravel. Finally, he neared the forest, and as he did so, he saw someone else walking along the path toward him. David couldn't take his eyes off the person, who exuded strength and dignity, goodness and intelligence, humor and kindness—and *life*. David simply knew all of this; somehow, he could just tell. And welling up in his chest he felt a sense of love, of longing, of recognition.

⋀⋀

How David came to be sitting on the garden bench with his grandfather, he didn't know. But there they were, relaxing among the flowers and trees, with a stream of water leaping and splashing along next to them, catching the sunshine, then falling into shadow. His grandfather put his hand on David's shoulder.

"It's good to see you, David."

"I thought you were dead, Grandpa."

The old man chuckled. "'Dead' isn't as dead as you might think."

"What is this place?"

"Don't you know?"

"Heaven?"

"You could call it that." His grandfather stretched his legs out in front of him.

"I'm dead too, then."

"Not exactly. You're sort of in between."

"What does that mean?"

"It means you'll have to go back. You still have work to do before you can stay here."

"It's just like in the stories."

"That's because the stories are true."

"Why am I here, then?"

"Because you have something to ask me."

David remembered his grandfather's transcript of the Book of Mormon characters—the Moroni Code—now long neglected. "That's right." he said. "I do."

"Go ahead."

"Why did you circle that character from the gold plates?"

"Since you came here to ask, you'd think I could tell you, wouldn't you? But I can't; you'll have to find out for yourself. If I just tell you, you won't learn what you need to learn. But I will tell you this: Don't just look at that character; look at its neighbors, too. And don't worry so much about what other people have said. Look at the characters for yourself—really *look* at them."

"All right. That's it?"

"For now." The old man patted David on the back.

"You mean there'll be more later?"

"There will be if you seek for it. Ask, seek, knock—remember?"

"Yes," David said. "I do."

"It's been wonderful to see you."

"You too, Grandpa." Suddenly David was choking up. He reached out to embrace this man he loved, and as he did so, a wave of exhaustion passed over him, then a wave of pain.

He closed his eyes. Then he opened them. A dim light shone somewhere above him, and a bank of machines was beeping softly near his bed. His shoulder throbbed with a dull pain, but he didn't seem to care much. What was he doing here? Hadn't he just been talking with his grandpa? He couldn't remember. Finally, tired of trying to think, he drifted off to sleep.

OCTOBER, 1834

〉⌐ ≋ ⼁⼁

Dear Brother,—

. . . I shall not attempt to paint to you the feelings of this heart, nor the majestic beauty and glory which surrounded us on this occasion; but you will believe me when I say, that earth, nor men, with the eloquence of time, cannot begin to clothe language in as interesting and sublime a manner as this holy personage. No; nor has this earth power to give the joy, to bestow the peace, or comprehend the wisdom which was contained in each sentence as they were delivered by the power of the Holy Spirit! Man may deceive his fellow man; deception may follow deception, and the children of the wicked one may have power to seduce the foolish and untaught, till nought but fiction feeds the many, and the fruit of falsehood carries in its current the giddy to the grave; but one touch with the finger of his love, yes, one ray of glory from the upper world, or one word from the mouth of the Savior, from the bosom of eternity, strikes it all into insignificance, and blots it forever from the mind! . . .

Oliver Cowdery

CHAPTER 27

For one of the few times in his life, Seth Pitt was afraid—terrified of being caught. After putting the Joseph Smith letter and its translation into a sidewalk mailbox, he'd dumped Tamara off on the side of the road, then taken Route 201 west to Tooele, where he pulled into the Wal-Mart parking lot, back in the shadows along the side of the store. He went inside, ignoring the greeter and detesting the fluorescent lights and the weirdly upbeat music. Walking quickly back to the automotive department, he grabbed six cans of black spray paint and a screwdriver. He paid for the merchandise with cash, and the woman at the checkout stand hardly looked up from her work. As he walked out the doors, he breathed a sigh of relief.

Back in the parking lot, he crept up to an old Chevrolet not far from his van—probably the car of a Wal-Mart employee. Suddenly he heard the bang of car doors, and loud voices. He crouched down low, waiting and watching, getting ready to run. But it wasn't the cops—just a couple of late-night customers, who disappeared into the store. He quickly went to work. With a few twists of the screwdriver, he removed the front license plate, then got back in his van and drove along the side streets until he reached the outskirts of town.

After a few more minutes of driving, he found what he was looking for—an abandoned farmhouse. He parked out back, and there, in the moonlight, he used the spray paint to give his old white van a new identity in black. It wasn't pretty, but it actually was an improvement, and the black paint wouldn't stand out in the darkness the way the white had done. He took off the old license plate and put on the new one. All of this took more time and trouble than he wanted, and he'd thought about just stealing a car somewhere along the line, but then the cops would be looking for that instead. *There's no justice,* he thought, now chugging along on I-80. He was headed for Reno, where he had some friends who might put him up for a while—maybe for a little cash or some drugs. If he kept up the pace, he could probably be there by morning.

But a few miles past Wendover, he could smell gas fumes seeping in through the air vents—not a good sign. And then he remembered—the drinking straw that stupid cop had wedged into the fuel line. He cursed, then pulled off onto the side of the road. But before he could stop, the engine compartment burst into flames in front of him. Unable to see, he stomped on the brakes, shut off the engine, and practically fell out of the van. But as he hurried around to the front, the whole thing exploded, the orange flames roaring into the night sky, and Seth found himself being propelled over the road and into the ditch in the median strip of the freeway, where he landed on his chest with an enormous thud.

At first he couldn't breathe—he thought he was dying. Then he realized he'd just had the wind knocked out of him, and as he calmed down, he was finally able to take in some air. He lay on the ground for several minutes, his eyes closed, not wanting to move. But he'd have to move eventually. After resting some more, he rose up on his hands and knees. He was hurt in several places—in the flickering light, he could see that his arms and chest were especially scraped up. He coughed, then spat out some blood. Putting his hand to his mouth, he found that his front teeth had been knocked out. *Oh, great,* he thought. He spat again, and pain shot through his jaws.

Gingerly, he tried to stand. The effort cost him, but he could do it. He brushed most of the gravel from his chest and arms. There was blood, although not as much as he'd feared. But the pain was excruciating.

He sat in the rocks and weeds on the side of the road, thinking about what to do. He could probably get along without medical care, but he needed to wash the dirt out of his wounds and rinse the blood from his mouth. He could hitch a ride back to Wendover; with his injuries and the still-burning shell of the van on the roadside, it wouldn't be hard to get a ride. Then he could clean himself up in a public restroom, maybe sleep in a park, and tomorrow he could hitchhike the rest of the way to Reno. And, he suddenly realized, he had to get going *now;* it wouldn't be long before the cops showed up to investigate the accident. And they'd be looking for the van's driver—a bit of a problem.

Maybe, he thought, *I should go back to Utah.* He turned the idea over in his mind. After finding the van, the police wouldn't be looking for him in Salt Lake; they'd probably be concentrating on the area around Wendover. It was an interesting thought.

But now his mouth was beginning to throb. He needed some painkillers—or booze—and maybe some bandages. Putting his hand to his bleeding gums, he felt a flood of anger. Nothing had worked out. Sonny was dead. And one person was responsible—that FBI agent. And then he realized—he really *was* going the wrong way. He didn't want to go to

Reno; he wanted to go back to Salt Lake—there were still some things he needed to do there. Gritting his remaining teeth, he limped up to the freeway—the eastbound side, heading back to Utah. It was time to even the score.

CHAPTER 28

⊁ ≋ ⊣ L

The sunlight streaming through the window woke David up. He was in bed, but certainly not his own—this one was far too uncomfortable—and he had an IV in his right arm and an oxygen tube under his nose. Several bouquets of flowers were sitting on the windowsill. Hadn't he just had a dream about flowers?

A heavy-set woman in a blue smock came through the door. "Well," she said, "you're awake. That's good!"

David still felt a little groggy. "Hi," he said sleepily, raising an index finger in greeting.

"My name's Marie," the nurse said. "I'll be going home in just a minute, as soon as Bob gets here to look after you."

"Bob?"

"He's the nurse on the day shift. He's good, but he's not nearly as gentle as I am." She laughed.

"What hospital is this?"

"LDS."

"Am I going to be all right?"

"Absolutely. We're taking good care of you."

"Thanks," David said. Then he remembered. "What day is it?"

"Friday. You slept all day yesterday. Of course, we gave you some help with that." The nurse smiled.

"Friday!" David groaned. He'd missed the deadline. He'd missed *everything*. He tried to roll over, but he couldn't—he'd been restrained. The effort brought a rush of pain.

"Don't try to move," the nurse said. "Your shoulder's pretty messed up."

"Don't worry," he said. He wasn't about to try that again. "Can I watch TV?"

"Sure. The remote is right there on the table."

David reached for the control with his left hand—his right one was bandaged across his chest. He turned on the television, then flipped through the channels, finally settling on an old *Perry Mason* episode, which he watched until the news came on. After a story about a hurricane, the scene shifted to some announcers with a picture of the Salt Lake Temple behind the newsdesk. "In local news," one of the announcers said, "leaders of The Church of Jesus Christ of Latter-day Saints revealed yesterday that the Church has been the victim of a blackmail attempt. The attempt involved a coded letter purportedly from Joseph Smith—one that may prove extremely damaging for the Church and its history. The blackmailers threatened to release the letter to the media unless the Church paid a ransom of ten million dollars—which the Church has refused to do. Church spokesman Wayne Underwood addressed members of the press yesterday afternoon at the Joseph Smith Memorial Building across from Temple Square."

The scene changed to the lobby of the Memorial Building, where Brother Underwood was standing at a podium, speaking into a microphone. "We do not yet know the meaning of this letter," he was saying, "but the Church will never capitulate to the demands of blackmailers. We have been working with the FBI to decipher the coded portion, so far without success. But whatever the full message might say, we are unafraid. This is the Lord's church, and his work will go forward.

"Many of us remember the forgeries perpetrated upon the Church during the 1980s, and it may be that this letter, too, is a forgery. We won't know until the blackmailers release the original document and it has been examined by experts. At that point, we'll give you an update." Brother Underwood smiled wryly. "We've learned a few things since Mark Hofmann."

The scene shifted back to the announcer at the newsdesk. "Today was the blackmailers' deadline for the Church to pay the ransom. Since the Church has refused to respond, we anticipate the release of the original letter at any time. Surprisingly, one of the blackmailers, Thornton Price, has already turned himself in to the authorities. He has identified the other blackmailers as Seth and Sonny Pitt, owners of a Salt Lake City bookstore specializing in rare books and documents."

The television showed a picture of the store.

"Sonny Pitt was killed Wednesday night in a gun battle with a law enforcement official at the Pioneer Memorial Museum; his brother, Seth, is still at large."

A mug shot of Seth appeared on the screen.

"Seth Pitt previously served a five-year prison term for fraud and manslaughter. He is armed and should be considered extremely dangerous. If you have any knowledge concerning the whereabouts of this man, please contact the police immediately. We'll keep you posted as further events in this important case unfold."

/\/\/\

After watching the news report, David slept for several hours until Bob, the nurse on the dayshift, woke him up. The man was huge, and obviously in good physical condition.

"You're a nurse?" David said.

"Yep." He had a deep voice, too.

"You're not very pretty."

"That's not what my wife says."

David laughed.

"Here's lunch—turkey sandwich, carrot sticks, carton of milk, and delicious cherry Jell-O. Just like in grade school."

"Yum," David said sarcastically. But actually, the food looked good, and he suddenly felt ravenously hungry. He tucked into the meal with a vengeance, although he had a little trouble eating the Jell-O with his left hand.

Later, after sleeping some more, he turned on the television for the six o'clock news. The program was already in progress; a reporter was standing in front of the LDS Church Office Building.

" . . . further developments in this fascinating story," the reporter said. "Salt Lake City television station ABC 4 has announced that they have received a package containing the original Joseph Smith letter held for ransom in the recent Church blackmail case."

A color photograph of the document appeared on the screen.

"The package also included a translation of the coded part of the letter, with an explanation of how it was deciphered. The station has released the text in full." The screen then scrolled through the lines as the reporter read them aloud:

Dear Brother:

It is with sensations of regret that I write these few lines in relation to the Book of Mormon. I cannot any longer forbear throwing off the mask, and letting you know the secret.

I have practised a deception in pretending to translate the

Book of Mormon through the medium of a seerstone, which never was the case. This you have long suspected, together with the conniving between the Witnesses and myself in relation to this matter.

I omit other important things which could I see you I could make you acquainted with.

Farewell untill I return,

Joseph Smith Jr.

"This could have an incredible impact on the LDS faithful," the reporter concluded. "Now back to you, Tracy." The camera moved back to the announcer in the studio, who looked grim. "We have with us Stephanie Carlson, head of Special Collections at the University of Utah's Marriott Library. Dr. Carlson, what do you think this letter will mean for members of The Church of Jesus Christ of Latter-day Saints?"

Dr. Carlson shook her head. "On its face, this letter will have serious repercussions. It implies that LDS founder Joseph Smith perpetrated a fraud in his account of the Book of Mormon translation, and that he conspired with the Three Witnesses to lie about the matter."

"Serious charges," the announcer said.

"Yes. Of course, the letter's authenticity has yet to be proven. I would encourage your viewers to suspend judgment on the matter until professionals have had a chance to fully examine the document."

The camera moved back to the announcer. "Thank you, Dr. Carlson. We've received word that local experts are presently looking over the letter, and that national experts are flying in to Salt Lake City. As important as this matter is for the LDS Church, we expect to hear initial opinions in the next day or two."

David was bowled over. If the letter was real . . .

Then he wondered about the translation—the message he

hadn't been able to figure out. How had they pulled it off? As soon as possible, he needed to get his hands on the explanation of how the letter had been deciphered. He felt an overwhelming urge to get back to work. But he doubted that he'd be doing that anytime soon.

CHAPTER 29

David's parents, along with his grandmother, visited him that evening, bringing still more flowers. They discussed the Joseph Smith letter, and David's father was almost gleeful about the whole affair. "I've always suspected that something like this would happen," he said. "Maybe this will finally bring people to their senses."

David's grandmother had the opposite opinion. "This is a test," she said. "You wait and see. That letter will turn out to be a forgery, and all you naysayers are going to look mighty foolish. I'll never give up my faith in Joseph Smith. Never."

David's mother didn't say anything. She'd long ago learned to keep out of her family's squabbles, which never seemed to settle anything.

"Personally," David said, "I just want to see how they decoded the letter. Maybe they got something wrong, and that's not what the letter says at all."

David's father snapped his fingers. "I knew there was something I wanted to bring you. There was an article about it in the newspaper."

"That's okay. They brought me a newspaper earlier. It didn't have enough information to tell me what I really need."

"I'll see what I can find out, then."

"Thanks, Dad. That'd be great."

David's mother put her hand on his forehead. "When will they let you go home?" she said. "Aren't you tired of being here?"

"They want to keep me one more day, just to make sure I'm okay. They're a little worried about infection, but so far there's no problem—I'm pumped too full of antibiotics and painkillers." David laughed. "It's really not so bad, but I wish the bed was more comfortable."

"I'm just so thankful you're going to be all right."

"Thanks, Mom." He knew what his mother was thinking—that he could easily have been killed.

/\/\/\

The next morning while David was finishing his breakfast, someone knocked on the door frame. He looked up. There was April, looking like springtime itself.

"April!" he said. "It's great to see you. Thanks for coming by."

"I can't stay long," she said. "And it's really not visiting hours yet. But I brought something I thought you might want." She handed David a sheet of paper. "It's a photocopy of the paper that explains how the Joseph Smith letter was decoded—along with a copy of the letter."

"Thank you! This is great."

"But David," she said, "if you're thinking the translation might be wrong, it's not. Pretty much anyone could follow the explanation."

David's face fell. "Why couldn't I figure it out, then?"

"You'll see. I'll leave you to it." She smiled, then turned to go.

"April?"

"Yes?" She turned back.

"Come again, okay?"

"You can count on it."

Long after she left, he was still smiling.

/\/\/\

All afternoon, David worked through the letter, sitting up in bed with the rolling hospital table tilted in front of him and the television turned on for major news announcements. He'd been right in his initial analysis of the pigpen code—it was just the garden-variety cipher. But the reason he hadn't been able to figure it out was simple: The code had been written sideways, and he'd been trying to read it as if it had been written right-side up, along with the rest of the letter. He felt mortified. But, he now realized, the problem had simply been caused by the peculiar nature of pigpen code. All of the symbols were symmetrical. So, if they were turned on their sides, they'd naturally be misread. He looked at the code as he'd initially tried to read it:

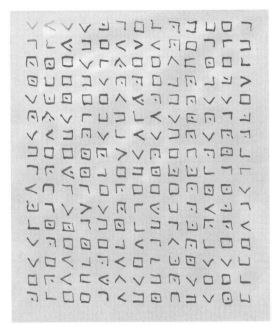

Then he turned it on its side.

He looked at the key.

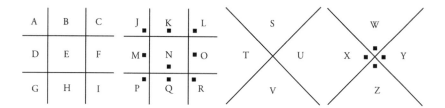

Now, sure enough, the whole thing made sense. What he'd thought was a G was really an I.

And what he'd thought was a D was an H.

And so on. No wonder the tricks with letter frequency and Caesar transpositions hadn't worked. He'd tried to make things way more complicated than they actually were. Evidently Joseph Smith and whoever he was writing to had, at some point, simply agreed to write and read their code sideways—something that must have proved very effective in hiding their messages. Writing awkwardly, he finished working out the translation:

ihavepractisedadeceptioninpretendingtotranslateth
bookofmormonthroughthemediumofaseerstonewhichnever
wasthecasethisyouhavelongsuspectedtogetherwithconniving
betweenthewitnessesandmyselfinrelationtothismatter

With spaces, punctuation, and capitalization, it would match the blackmailers' translation exactly:

I have practised a deception in pretending to translate the Book of Mormon through the medium of a seerstone, which never was the case. This you have long suspected, together with the conniving between the Witnesses and myself in relation to this matter.

Vaguely, he wondered how the blackmailers had managed to get it. They'd probably had help—or maybe just plenty of time to work on it.

Just then the television announced "breaking news," as the reporter called it. "LDS historian and handwriting expert Richard James has released a preliminary report on the Joseph Smith letter. His analysis confirms that the handwriting is definitely that of LDS Church's founder. Dr. James, how did you arrive at your conclusion?"

The camera shifted to a balding, middle-aged man wearing wire-rimmed glasses.

"Normal handwriting is actually a subconscious process," he said, "which makes a perfect forgery almost impossible. Forgers have to think about things like letter forms, slant, and size, all at the same time. That means most forgers write slowly, with a lot of starts and stops—and that can be detected by examining the ink under a magnifying glass or a microscope. We don't see that in this document."

"But Doctor, couldn't a forger practice writing in Joseph Smith's style until it became subconscious?"

"Yes, that is possible. But that kind of thing is rare. Most forgers don't have the skill—or the patience—to do it. In addition, there's the wording of the letter, which is definitely the kind of language Joseph Smith used. We don't talk—or write—like that anymore, so that would also be difficult for a forger to duplicate."

"What will happen next?"

"On Monday, a team of experts will gather at the University of Utah, where they'll be examining the physical characteristics of the document—the age of the paper, the chemical composition of the ink, and so forth."

"Dr. James, thanks for your analysis." The camera moved back to the announcer. "We'll be bringing you additional information as soon as it becomes available. Now we return to our regular programming."

David wondered what the experts would decide. Could anyone ever know for sure? Then he thought about the letter's ramifications for the Church. Surely it had to be a forgery, despite these latest findings. And, in his heart, that's what he found himself hoping.

CHAPTER 30

〉ᶜ ≋ ᆉ E

After catching a ride back to Wendover, Seth cleaned himself up at a gas station, cut off his ponytail with his pocketknife, and, as best he could, took care of his injuries. Then he lay low for a few days, sleeping under the trees at a golf course and hiding out during the day, recuperating and planning his next move. Finally, when most of his pain had subsided, he hitchiked back to Tooele, where he caught UTA bus 75 on Main Street. He rode the bus for the half-hour trip to 8400 West in Magna, a small community at the far west of the Salt Lake Valley, then got off and walked several blocks north until he came to a tiny house on the east side of the road, surrounded by trees and bushes and set far back on the lot, away from other homes in the area. The house was gray—not from paint, but from the effects of the weather on the bare, rough boards knocked together to make walls. The unkempt yard was full of weeds, and wild morning glory covered the wire fence that surrounded it, the small, white blossoms adding a touch of unintentional beauty to the dilapidated home.

Seth pushed open the little gate and walked up to the ragged screen door, through which he could hear the drone of the television. He knocked, loudly, and after a few moments a woman came to the door. Her hair was long, streaked with gray, and she wore a low-cut white blouse and tight jeans, accentuating her spindly body. At first, unaccustomed to the light, she couldn't see who was standing there. Then her eyes widened.

"Hi, Ma," Seth said.

"Oh, Seth," she said. "You can't come here."

"No place else to go." He pulled open the door, pushed past her, and sprawled onto the sagging couch. "I've been hurt, Ma." He held out his arms, drew back his lips.

"I don't care; I'll call the cops."

"No, you won't." Seth looked at her fiercely.

"You're threatening your own mother?"

Seth sighed. "I'm not going to hurt you, Ma."

"You bet you're not," she said. "I already took enough of that from your father—God rest his rotten soul." She sat down in her old wooden rocker and stared stoically at nothing.

"It's okay, Ma. There's something I need to take care of. And . . . uh . . . well, I wanted to see you."

His mother looked at him quizzically. "What are you up to?"

"I just need to stay a few weeks—lay low until the heat's off. Please. I can give you some money . . ."

"I don't want your money," she said sharply. Then she shook her head. "You can stay, I guess—maybe do a few chores, pay for some groceries. But the cops have already been here looking for you. If they come around again, I won't protect you; I'll say you forced me to let you stay, and I'll expect you to back up that story. I'm not getting arrested for aiding and abetting."

"Thanks, Ma. There's one more thing."

"What?"

"I want to pay my respects to Sonny."

"Well, he's up on the hill. You can take my bicycle if you want to go up there." She paused. "How did it happen, Seth?"

"It was an accident, Ma."

She shook her head. "I read the paper; it didn't have to be that way."

"I know. I'm so sorry."

She wiped her eyes. "Go on," she said. "Go see him. I'll have something for you to eat when you get back."

/\/\/\

Seth rode the creaky blue bicycle across the highway, onto land owned by Kennecott Copper. The road leading up to the graveyard was too steep to ride, so he walked the bike up to the summit and then leaned it against the sign reading "Pleasant Green Cemetery." But the place was anything but green and pleasant. Sagebrush grew around the perimeter, and many of the burial plots were choked with weeds. There was no grass—nor any way to water it if there had been. Not far from the cemetery entrance, Seth located a pine board set into the dusty soil. His mother had written on it carefully with a marking pen:

GERALD "SONNY" PITT
LOVING SON
1968–2007

The board wasn't much, but his mother couldn't afford a stone, and it looked better than some of the other markers— a piece of sandstone someone had inscribed with a nail, and a rough wooden cross with painted letters. Next to Sonny's grave was a small metal plaque embedded in a concrete slab:

JOSHUA PITT
1940–2002

Seth scuffed his foot in the dirt. "Rest in peace, Pa," he said. "You old cuss." But looking at Sonny's grave, he didn't know what to say. He stood there a long time, thinking.

When they were kids, Seth, three years older than Sonny, had always taken care of his little brother. Seth remembered coming home from school on a winter's day to find two other kids tormenting Sonny. He'd been making a snowman, and the bullies had pushed it over, then pulled the knit cap off Sonny's head and tossed it back and forth, just out of Sonny's reach, laughing and taunting until he was hysterical with rage and fear. Always a big kid, Seth had picked up the bullies by the scruff of the neck, pushed their faces into a snowbank, and then kicked them halfway down the block before letting them go. "Don't you *ever* bother my brother again," he'd yelled after them. And they hadn't—nor had anyone else.

Now, Seth could hardly believe that Sonny was gone—and that it was Seth's own bullet that had killed the little brother he'd always tried to protect. But he couldn't let himself think about that. It wasn't his fault anyway. "Good-bye, Sonny," he finally said. Then he paused. "I might not be back again."

In his mind, he went over the events of the past few weeks, remembering everything that had gone wrong. He felt the sorrow welling up inside him, but he didn't want that. With a sob, he pushed it down, filling its place with white-hot anger, the blinding rage he'd need to finish what he'd come back to do.

CHAPTER 31

⊃ ⼬ ≋ ⼦

In a specially outfitted lab at the Marriott Library at the University of Utah, the forensic document experts had been hard at work all morning, testing the authenticity of the coded Joseph Smith letter. Now they were going over their findings to see if anything had been overlooked. The head of the team, Mark Horowitz, a member of the American Board of Forensic Examiners from New York City, was holding the letter over a light table, examining the paper with a magnifying glass. Other members of the team were standing around the table, looking on. "The paper looks right," he said. "You can see a foolscap watermark here." He pointed with his white-gloved index finger. "And you can see that this is laid paper. Of course, it's common for forgers to create new documents on old paper."

"How do the edges look?" The question came from Linda Burston, a forensic chemist from Chicago.

"This thing is in such bad shape it's hard to tell much. But it's safe to say the paper hasn't been cut during modern times—by a razor blade, for instance. So it's not something a forger has cut from an old book or something like that." He put down the magnifying glass. "I'm saying the paper is authentic."

"Same thing on the ink," Linda said. "We used PIXE for the analysis, and it's just plain old iron gallotannic. Under ultraviolet light, there's no hazing or any sign of cracking or running."

"What caused all the staining?"

Linda smiled. "Really strong coffee."

Everyone laughed.

"And beef gravy."

"Well, that's disgusting," Mark said.

"That's what happens when you read at the dinner table."

The group laughed again.

"What do we have on the letter's provenance?" Mark asked.

"Nothing certain." Linda shook her head. "Blackmailers, remember? Thornton Price claims he picked it up in Kirtland, but we can't trust his story."

"Right. So we've got to be doubly careful. Is there any way the ink could have been artificially aged?"

"Well, as I said, I don't see anything under ultraviolet light to indicate that."

"How about infrared?"

"We saw no reason to use infrared," Linda said. "All it would show is if different inks had been used."

"Would that tell us if the letter had been altered during the 1800s?"

The room was suddenly quiet.

"You mean someone could have been trying to make Joseph Smith look bad way back then? By adding or changing words or letters?"

"Right."

"Yes, infrared would definitely show that. That's a very interesting idea." Her face lit up. "Think how easy it would be to add a dot or a line to some of those pigpen characters. That could change everything!"

Mark smiled with satisfaction.

"Let's check it right now." Linda switched on the Polylight machine.

CHAPTER 32

$\Rightarrow^c \approx \dashv\mathord{\uparrow}$

As she walked up the long ramp and entered the reception area of the Salt Lake County Metro Jail, Tamara was mortified. She'd never been inside a jail before, and she certainly wasn't comfortable with the idea of sitting next to the kind of people who were lounging around the stark, concrete-walled room on hard benches, waiting to visit the inmates.

After signing in with a uniformed guard, she was instructed to put her purse and anything metal into a locker, and after a few minutes she and the group that had gathered were ushered through a metal detector and into another plain room to wait until the appointed time for their visits.

Many of those who were waiting looked pretty rough, as if they'd spent time in jail themselves. A few of the others seemed to be family members who appeared to feel as out of place as she did. She just wanted to talk with Thornton and get out.

She sat on a bench near a girl with purple hair, a spike through her bottom lip, and a black T-shirt with bold red letters that read "Left for Dead"—evidently the name of some local rock band.

"Hi," the girl said. "My name's Tasha."

Tamara didn't know what to say. She thought about

"Pleased to meet you," but that certainly wasn't accurate. "I'm Tamara," she finally said. Then she paused. "I . . . really don't feel comfortable here."

"You'll get used to it," the girl said.

"I don't want to 'get used to it.'" Tamara glared. "I shouldn't even be here."

"You know," the girl said, "I come here like clockwork to see my boyfriend—he got busted for selling crack. And I see people like you all the time—people who think they're above all this because they wear nice clothes and drive expensive cars. But the truth is, we're all in this together. Maybe you'll get that when your guy comes out in that orange jumpsuit—just like everybody else. Probably your husband, right? Or your brother?"

"My husband." Tamara's lips were set.

"What did he do?"

"He didn't do *anything*. He's not that kind of person."

The girl rolled her eyes. "Whatever."

"This is all a mistake." Tamara got up and moved to a different part of the room, as far from the girl as possible. The girl glanced over at her, gave her a look that Tamara had a hard time deciphering—it seemed to be a mixture of smugness and contempt.

After a few minutes, a guard announced the time for the visit, and Tamara and the rest of the group filed out into a long corridor leading to the holding areas. An electronically activated door allowed Tamara to enter a narrow room with five visiting stations, and she sat down on a metal stool in front of a thick glass window and waited. Then a heavy metal door slid open, and Thornton walked into the visiting area on the other side of the glass. He *was* wearing one of those awful orange jumpsuits, and he needed a shave. When he spotted Tamara at one of the stations, he came quickly and sat on a stool facing her. There were no phones, and the people on both sides of Tamara were talking loudly in order to be heard.

At first Tamara couldn't speak. Finally, she asked, "What happened, Thornton? Why are you in here?"

He shook his head.

"Did you really do the things they're saying on the news?"

"I did a lot of things."

Tamara felt the fear, the anger, rising, filling her up. Then she started to cry.

Thornton went on. "I gave Sonny and Seth the letter they used to blackmail the Church."

"Why? What would make you do such a thing?"

"They forced me."

"They put a gun to your head?"

Now Thornton choked up. "I stole documents from the Church and sold them—they threatened to turn me in."

"Oh, Thornton. Why would you do such a thing?"

"I didn't think the Church would even notice. I thought I was making a better life for us—for you and me."

She shook her head, wiped the tears from her face. "Couldn't you find a way to make money honestly?"

"I don't know. We're so far in debt, and—"

"And that's my fault, right?" Her eyes blazed.

He looked at her intently, unflinchingly. "Yes, it is. It's something you have to change. And it's time I finally said so." He paused. "But it's my fault too—just as much as yours. We've always had to look good to everyone else; we've always had to be the perfect couple. We've fed that in each other. And we have to stop."

Tamara was crying hard now. Finally she choked out, "I thought you were a good person. I thought you could do great things. I've always encouraged you. And you blame me?

I'm not the thief. I'm not the blackmailer." She got up to leave.

"Tamara, please don't go. Please, just stay and talk to me."

"There's nothing to talk about."

Thornton put his head in his hands. "This is why I couldn't tell you," he sobbed. "I knew I'd lose you. And I'll die if I lose you." He looked up, the tears streaming down his face. "I love you, Tamara. You know I do."

Tamara didn't say anything. The room was a blur. She wiped her eyes, trying to get hold of herself. Leaving Thornton at the window, she walked to the door leading out of the visiting area, but she didn't know how to activate it. As she glanced back at the visiting stations, the girl with purple hair turned to watch her, this time with a look of understanding, of sympathy. But Tamara didn't want sympathy; she just wanted out of this horrible place. And when the door finally clicked open, she hurried into the corridor and, finally, out into the night.

CHAPTER 33

꙰ ≋ ⼻ □

David was sitting in his hospital room, watching the news. He'd had one more visit from April the day before. Now, on Tuesday morning, he was more than ready to go home, and his parents would be arriving any minute to pick him up. He wanted to go back to his apartment, but they'd insisted that he stay with them for a few days, just until he was back on his feet. He smiled. They really did love him—and each other, in spite of their differences about the Church.

On the television, the reporter was standing in the lobby of the Marriott Library at the University of Utah, where the forensic document team was about to announce their findings about the Joseph Smith letter. David had no doubt that the entire city was watching—possibly the entire state and beyond.

"Here are the examiners now," the reporter said. The team filed into the lobby, looking tired but alert, and seated themselves at a long table.

Mark Horowitz, seated in the center, pulled the microphone closer. "Thanks for your patience," he said. "We've examined the Joseph Smith letter in every detail, using the most advanced technology available. Here are our findings." He pulled a sheet of paper out of his pocket, then smiled wanly. "I'm going to read them; I don't want to get anything wrong."

The crowd laughed nervously. Just then David's parents came in. He hugged them both. "You're just in time for the big announcement," he whispered.

"The handwriting is authentic," Mark read. "It is smooth and fluid, with no sign of irregularities, and it is consistent with the writing of Joseph Smith.

"The language is authentic; it is consistent with the kind of language Joseph Smith used in other letters.

"The paper is authentic; it is consistent with paper from the time of Joseph Smith and has not been cut or otherwise modified in modern times.

"The ink is authentic; it is consistent with an iron gallotannic recipe that was commonly used during Joseph Smith's time, and it has not been artificially aged.

"Finally, the ink is uniform; it has not been added to or modified after the letter was written. At first we thought the letter might have been altered, but infrared analysis proves otherwise.

"In summary, our unanimous conclusion is that this document is in no way a forgery; it is precisely what it appears to be—an authentic letter written by Joseph Smith, the founder of the LDS Church."

He looked up from the paper. "We will now take questions." The questions were predictable, casting no new light on what had been said. David and his parents sat stunned. None of them said a word. Finally David switched off the television and got his things. All he wanted to do was go home, where everything was familiar, everything was stable. Certainly the world would never be the same again.

/\/\/\

All afternoon, David and his parents watched the news, and there was plenty to choose from, with announcers, commentators, and pundits expounding on nearly every channel. On the *Barry Prince Show*, the dapper host was interviewing the well-known Mormon-watcher Jodie Baxter.

"Jodie," Barry said, "what direction do you see the Mormon Church taking, with these new revelations (pardon the pun) about Joseph Smith? Will the Church fall apart, or will it keep going?"

"I suspect," Jodie said, her fingers interlaced, "that the Church will keep going—but not without a lot of fallout. Already today we've seen several well-known Mormons leaving the Church, and I'm sure there'll be more. As for the Church's future—well, over the past few decades, we've seen a greater emphasis on Jesus Christ and a moving away from a focus on Joseph Smith, and I believe that trend will continue, but now with greater acceleration. The Church will become more like the mainstream Christian faiths. Certainly this is what we've seen with the Community of Christ."

Barry pushed his glasses up onto his nose, then ran his fingers through his thinning brown hair. "You say that the Church has been moving away from Joseph Smith. I'll bet if you asked the 'Mormon on the street,' so to speak, he'd say that's not true."

"Maybe the average Mormon would say it's not true, but I calls 'em as I sees 'em, Barry. And in Mormon meetings over the past few decades, that's been the trend."

"Isn't that a good thing?"

"Most evangelicals would say yes. But really, the Mormons have never 'worshiped' Joseph Smith in the way critics think. There's no need to choose between Jesus Christ and Joseph Smith. The analogy is closer to what we see in Islam—Jesus is

God and Joseph is his prophet. And of course, that's what the Mormons have always said: 'We thank thee, O God, for a prophet.'"

"Interesting. But now, with this letter, that's likely to change."

"Yes. And in my opinion, that's a real tragedy. Joseph Smith taught a number of distinctive doctrines that set the Church apart from other religious organizations—things like a premortal life, Heavenly Parents, the sealing of families for eternity, and the possibility that mortals can become gods. If the Church loses those doctrines, what does it have to offer? Nothing more than any other church."

"Where can you get a steak when all the restaurants are owned by McDonald's?"

"Exactly—although there's nothing wrong with McDonald's."

"What about the Church's claim to authority? It will still have that."

"Every church claims authority, in one way or another. Nothing unique there."

"Do you think these 'distinctive doctrines,' as you call them, have anything to do with the Church's phenomenal growth over the past few decades?"

"Of course they do. These are the kinds of things that resonate in people's souls, that offer an explanation of the meaning of life."

"You almost sound like a believer."

Jodie smiled and shook her head. "I'm an agnostic. But I like to think I'm a good observer."

∧⋁∧

Finally the station announced what David—and probably everyone else—had been waiting for: "We interrupt this program to bring you an official statement from Grant W. Iverson, president of The Church of Jesus Christ of Latter-day Saints." As David waited, he realized he was holding his breath. He forced himself to exhale. Finally the camera showed President Iverson sitting behind a big walnut desk, evidently in his office in the Church Administration Building.

"To all who may be listening," the president said, "and especially to members of The Church of Jesus Christ of Latter-day Saints and our many friends around the world, I send my love and my greeting.

"With the release of this coded Joseph Smith letter, our critics are predicting our demise. But this is nothing new; they've made that prediction since the Church's beginnings.

"It is true that this letter looks damaging. But I say to you, in the name of Israel's God, that there is more to this than meets the eye. We have not seen the end of this. And to any who are concerned or confused, we say, 'Wait on, hold on, for the arm of the Lord to be revealed.' And until that happens, we will do what we have always done in times of crisis." The president lifted his hand. "Carry on! Carry on! Carry on!"

/\/\/\

All evening the television showed more—pundits analyzing President Iverson's statement, closet doubters finally renouncing their membership, critics gleefully predicting the Church's downfall, statements of sympathy and support from leaders of other churches. Finally David stood up. "I'm tired," he said. "And I think I've heard enough for one day. I guess I'll pack it in."

"It looks like your dad already has." David's mother nodded over at his father, who was snoring lightly in his big recliner. "Sleep tight. And if you need anything, let me know."

"Thanks, Mom." David kissed his mother on the forehead,

then climbed the stairs to his old bedroom. His mother had turned it into a sewing room, but his bed was still in place, along with his nightstand. He switched on the dusty reading lamp, then undressed and got under the covers. Everything seemed so familiar, and yet everything had changed.

He remembered so clearly the night when his dad had caught him reading. "The Book of Mormon is full of mistakes," his father had said. "Don't you think God should be able to spell?"

Now David knew the answer to that question. In spite of President Iverson's attempt at damage control, God didn't write the book; Joseph Smith did—and he really wasn't a very good speller. David smiled at that, but inside he felt empty, as if his heart had stopped beating, its familiar rhythm stilled. "When I became a man, I put away childish things," his father had quoted from Paul. Now, David knew, his childhood was over; it was time to grow up. But he wasn't happy about it.

PART THREE

CHAPTER 34

On Monday, ten days after the shooting, David went back to work. His shoulder was still giving him some trouble, but it was healing well, and he was starting to feel like his old self again. Wilcox and some of the other agents had made a bit of a fuss over him, with balloons and a welcome-back sign, but David didn't want a fuss; he still felt terrible that he hadn't been able to work out the code on the Joseph Smith letter—even though it really wouldn't have made any difference in the end. Another thing was that Seth was still at large—and nobody was happy about that.

To David's surprise, and despite the critics' predictions, the Church was still standing. A number of Latter-day Saints had quietly—or not so quietly—resigned their membership, but the majority had still gone to their meetings the day before, carrying on in faith, just as President Iverson had asked them to do. David admired their resolve, but he had to wonder a little about their sanity. After all, the letter was what it was; there was no getting around that.

David's father had said surprisingly little about the whole affair. After his initial caustic remarks, he'd kept quiet, just reading his evening newspaper like always. David's mother wasn't saying anything either, but David could tell that her heart had been broken. His grandmother, on the other hand, was still adamant in her refusal to accept the letter's implications. She wasn't in denial; she simply knew that Joseph Smith was a prophet, and that was that.

There was one thing David was having a hard time reconciling, however. As he'd read the Book of Mormon off and on throughout his life, he'd been able to see patterns and connections in the text, subtleties that shouldn't have been there if someone had just made the whole thing up. And why go to all that trouble? If someone wanted to set up a religion, a pamphlet would have done the job. At first David had simply accepted the letter's dismal conclusions. But now, looking at the bigger picture, he wasn't sure what to think. He suspected that a lot of other people felt the same way—maybe that's why the Church was still going.

As David thought about all this, there was one part of the whole experience that stood out from the rest, one that he couldn't get out of his mind—April. He hadn't talked to her since she'd visited him in the hospital. And that, he decided, needed to change.

⁄\/\/\

David had often faced hazardous duty, but right now he was terrified. He picked up the phone. Then he put it down. Then he picked it up again. It wasn't that he didn't think April would go out with him; it was just that he didn't know how to ask her. Finally he dialed the number, deciding to say whatever came naturally; that was probably the best approach.

"Hi, April," he said as she picked up. "This is David."

"David who?"

"David Hunter."

"Oh, *that* David." She laughed.

"You already knew who it was, didn't you."

"I do have caller ID."

"Oh, right. Um, it's nice to hear your voice, April."

"Yes, I'll go out with you—and it took you long enough to ask."

"I haven't asked yet."

"A picnic? That sounds wonderful. I'll make sandwiches and everything."

David looked at the phone. "Are you talking to somebody else?"

"No, David. Just you."

"Okay . . ."

"Saturday? That sounds great. Pick me up at noon—7372 Meadow Lane."

"Uh, all right. I will. Thanks!"

He hung up the phone. *Well*, he thought, *that was easy.* Then he started to laugh. What was he getting himself into here? He didn't know—but he was already starting to like it.

When David picked April up, she'd said they were going to Lamb's Canyon—a place David had heard of but never visited. But, with April as navigator, he'd driven up Parley's Canyon and then exited onto a narrow road squeezed between two hillsides covered with pine, aspen, and scrub oak, with a stream running down the side of the road and picnic tables sequestered among the trees. The place was beautiful, and April had brought a thermos full of lemonade and an old-fashioned picnic basket with egg-salad sandwiches, potato chips, and pickles, with an apple pie carefully placed on the side. David was impressed, and the sandwiches were great.

"These are *good*," David said, his mouth full of food.

"Our neighbors have chickens," April said. "Those free-range eggs make all the difference."

"I'll say." He munched down a pickle. Then he had a

thought. "I don't mean to be nosy," he said, "but, uh, do you have a boyfriend or anything like that?"

April laughed, then fluttered her eyelids. "Why, no, David. Why do you ask?"

"Well, a pretty girl like you . . . I mean . . ."

"You asked me out because you think I'm pretty?"

"Well, no—I mean yes . . ." David smiled and shook his head. "Do you torture all your dates like this?"

"Of course." April laughed. "Although I haven't had too many dates lately."

"Why not?"

"I dated a lot at Utah State, but after I graduated, I started working at the Church Office Building. The dating scene there isn't exactly smoking hot."

David laughed. "I see."

"And what about you?" April asked. "Girlfriends galore?"

"Not right now. I was engaged once, though."

"Really? What happened?"

"She decided she didn't want to marry someone who might get shot during a typical day at work."

April shook her head. "I can understand that. But some-body's got to do the job. Right?"

"Absolutely."

"David, listen. I've been wanting to get your reaction to the big news."

He groaned. "I'm having such a good time. Do we *have* to talk about that?"

"We do sometime."

"Later, okay?"

"All right. But at least tell me how the work on your grandfather's transcript is going."

"Honestly, I've never gotten back to it."

"But you're going to, right?"

He shook his head. "I don't know. After everything that's happened, is there really any point?"

"Your grandpa seemed to think so."

"I suppose he did." After all this time, David still missed the old man. And as he thought of him, something tugged at his memory. It had been months since his grandfather had died, and yet it seemed like he'd talked with him recently—something about flowers. But that couldn't be right. A dream, maybe?

"You should keep on with it—if only to find out what he was thinking."

David shook his head. "I don't know."

"There's that circled character." She smiled knowingly, then tilted her head.

"Yeah."

"You do like a challenge."

"True."

"I'll help you."

"Hmm. That is tempting." He took a drink of lemonade.

"Good. Monday. Historical Library. Lunchtime. Bring your grandfather's transcript."

He rolled his eyes. "All right." Actually, the idea felt good. Maybe life *could* get back to normal—or even better.

CHAPTER 35

ᗒᶠ ≋ ᐩᗩ ⊐

As promised, David met April at the Church Historical
Library the following Monday at noon, bringing
along his grandfather's transcript of the Book of
Mormon characters. She was ready to get back to their original
research, but David had other ideas.

"I've had enough of trying to match the characters to
existing languages," he said, "or reading what other people
have said about them." He smiled. "We've been calling this a
code; maybe it's time we started treating it like one."

"Sounds fine," April said. "What do we do?"

"First, let's make some enlarged copies of the transcript.
Then let's cut one of the copies into pieces—one character per
piece."

This took a lot longer than they thought it would—there
were 216 characters, and some of them were tiny, even on the
enlarged photocopy. Finally, David said, "Now let's put the
repeated characters together."

"What are we trying to do?"

"We want to see how many times each character is used."

"Letter frequency—like with the pigpen code."

"Right."

But figuring out the character frequency turned out to be
harder than it looked. Sometimes it was impossible to know

whether a symbol was unique or just a variation on an existing character.

In the end, they just did the best they could, hoping to sort out any mistakes later.

"Okay," April said when they were finished. "But now what?"

"Good question. It's not like English, where we know that the most-used letter is E."

"Right."

"But we could see which characters usually show up together."

"What good would that do?"

David smiled. "I have no idea. But you never know where something might lead. Sometimes you just have to try something and see what happens. You can't always figure things out ahead of time."

"Like riding a bicycle," April said.

"Exactly."

"You go forward with faith."

David looked at her quizzically. "Well, I never thought about it like that before. But yes, I guess that's right."

They started in again with the cut-up pieces but soon found the combinations far too complex to handle.

"This isn't working," April said.

"No, it's not. Any ideas?"

"When the going gets tough, the tough get a computer."

"Hmm."

"We could use a regular letter or number to stand for each symbol. Then we could manipulate the letters and numbers on-screen rather than trying to work with these pieces of paper."

"Brilliant. Can we use your computer?"

"We can use my laptop. I bring it for meetings and stuff."

"Speaking of meetings . . ." David looked at his watch. "I need to get back to work. But lunchtime tomorrow?"

"Sure. I'll bring sandwiches."

"Egg salad?"

April laughed. "You really liked those, didn't you."

"Mmmm-hmm."

"Okay. We'll take the laptop and eat at the tables on the plaza, east of the temple."

"Sounds great." He started to leave but then turned back. "April?"

"Yes?"

"Thanks for helping me with this."

She gave him a dazzling smile. "My pleasure."

CHAPTER 36

⊁ ≋ ⊬

The next day, when David got to the plaza east of the temple, the flowers were blooming, and people were lounging and visiting on the benches around the reflecting pool, enjoying the sunshine. April was sitting at one of the wrought-iron tables, with a sack full of sandwiches, and she was already starting to work things out on her laptop.

"Well, you're efficient," he said as he sat down.

"Thanks! I just think this is so interesting."

"That's one of the things I like about you—along with these sandwiches." He unwrapped one and started to eat.

"Wouldn't it be great if we really could figure this out?"

"I doubt there's anything to it," he said. "But maybe we can work out what my grandpa was thinking."

"Wow. That Joseph Smith letter really got to you, didn't it."

David rolled his eyes. "So we *are* going to talk about this."

"Don't you think we should?"

"I guess so. I just don't know what to think. Joseph Smith admitted he lied about translating the Book of Mormon. For me, that pretty much settles it. But when I read the book, something about it grabs me, you know? It's deep, and it's complex. It seems like there's more going on there than if someone just made it up. But maybe I'm just reading things into it."

"Like how?"

David thought a minute, then looked up at the temple. "A while ago I walked through Temple Square on my way to work. On the main spire, on the back of the temple, there's a carving of the Big Dipper. Have you noticed that?"

"Yes," she said. "It represents the priesthood, I think—pointing the way home."

"Well, see, there's the thing. I was thinking that if we were on some other planet, those stars wouldn't line up the same way. From that point of view, it wouldn't even be the Big Dipper anymore. It wouldn't represent *anything*."

"And?"

"And I'm wondering if the patterns I see in the Book of Mormon are the same kind of thing—I don't see them because they're really *there*, but just because of the things I'm interested in, the things I like to think about."

"Like seeing a face in the cracks on a wall."

"Exactly."

April sighed. "That's deep."

"The human mind is made to see patterns. And I've always been good at that; that's one of the reasons I became a cryptographer."

"That makes sense. But when you decipher something, you do get a message, right? One that someone *meant* to communicate."

"That's true." David paused, thinking. "So how can you know the difference? How can you know if a pattern was made on purpose, or if it's just an accident?"

April thought for a moment. "I'd say you have to look at the whole wall. Maybe you can make out a face somewhere, but if there are lots of other cracks that don't look like anything, that's a clue that the 'face' is just accidental."

"Hmm."

"But if there are *lots* of faces on the wall—lots of patterns that seem to make sense—they're probably there on purpose. Together they show a 'preponderance of evidence,' if you see what I mean."

"I see you've been watching too much *Law and Order* on television." He smiled. "But you could be right."

She pointed to a copy of the Book of Mormon transcript. "So what do you think? Do these characters look like they were arranged on purpose?"

"Well, that's what we're trying to figure out, I guess. Of course, Joseph Smith could have just made the characters up."

"If that's what you really think, you won't get anywhere. You have to try some things, remember? You have to go forward with faith, just like President Iverson said."

David started to smile. "You're good."

"There's one more thing."

"What?"

She paused. "Have you prayed about this?"

David lowered his head. "Not really."

"In the end, that's the only way to find out for sure, David."

He looked up, his eyes moist. "I've heard that my whole life."

"But you've never really done it?"

He shook his head.

"Then there's your assignment."

"You're awfully bossy for such a pretty girl."

April laughed. "I'll tell you what," she said. "Let's go to Lamb's Canyon again this weekend."

"That sounds great!"

"But no food."

David's face fell.

"We'll fast. And while we're up there, we'll pray."

"I don't know, April. It's such a personal thing."

"Or—you could do it on your own."

He smiled. "That doesn't sound so good either."

"Well, you decide, and then let me know. But I'll tell you what I'm going to do."

"What's that?"

"I'm going to pray—for you. And I'm going to keep on believing. I know there's more to this than we think."

FEBRUARY, 1835

Dear Brother—

. . . Our brother was urged forward and strengthened in the determination to know for himself of the certainty and reality of pure and holy religion—And it is only necessary for me to say, that while this excitement continued, he continued to call upon the Lord in secret for a full manifestation of divine approbation, and for, to him, the all important information, if a Supreme being did exist, to have an assurance that he was accepted of him. This, most assuredly, was correct—it was right. The Lord has said, long since, and his word remains steadfast, that to him who knocks it shall be opened, and whosoever will, may come and partake of the waters of life freely. . . .

Oliver Cowdery

CHAPTER 37

꒷ ≋ ꓕ Ⲉ

When David went home to his apartment that night, he really didn't feel like eating. At first he told himself he just wasn't hungry—too many of those sandwiches, maybe. But as the evening wore on, with nothing to eat and nothing to drink, he had to admit he was fasting.

He turned on the television, surfed through the channels, but everything seemed so garish, so shallow, so noisy. Finally, he went out on the balcony and watched the sun go down behind the Oquirrh Mountains. Usually sunsets made him feel sad, but tonight, as he watched the golden clouds, the wheeling seagulls, the whole world seemed at peace.

When the sky finally turned dark, he went back inside and switched on the table lamp, then picked up his battered paperback copy of the Book of Mormon—the same one he'd read as a teenager. He turned to his old friend, Moroni, and read the familiar words:

"And when ye shall receive these things, I would exhort you that ye would ask God, the Eternal Father, in the name of Christ, if these things are not true; and if ye shall ask with a sincere heart, with real intent, having faith in Christ, he will manifest the truth of it unto you, by the power of the Holy Ghost."

But this time, it was the next verse that struck him:

"And by the power of the Holy Ghost ye may know the truth of all things."

The truth of all things. That was the answer—if the Book of Mormon was true. But was it?

He knelt by the couch, knowing his own sincerity, his real intent. But faith—that he did not have. At least not much.

He thought of all that had happened over the past few weeks, of his prayer in the darkness, of his climb up the stairs with the tiny flashlight, of how narrowly he'd avoided death. Was that all just accidental?

"Father in heaven," he prayed. "Thank you for saving my life. Thank you for my family. Thank you for April. And please—I need to know. I really do." His voice broke. "I'm sorry I'm so ignorant and so faithless. Please forgive me. Bless me to know the truth."

But now, he couldn't go on; he couldn't say anything more. And suddenly he felt exhausted, as if all the events of the past few weeks had finally settled onto his shoulders. Finally, without receiving an answer, he went to bed.

Over the next several days, David continued to pray, but now a new question kept coming up in his mind: Even if he got an answer, how would he know the answer was real and not just an emotional response or his own subconscious reaction to his fervent pleading? Would he have to pray again to know if the *answer* was true? And then again to know if *that* answer was true? Where would it ever end? He knew that this kind of thinking was getting him nowhere, but he couldn't keep it out of his mind. It was almost as if someone was toying with him, taunting him, trying to fill him with confusion. How could he ever really *know?* And with that very question on his lips, on Sunday night he fell asleep, still kneeling by the side of his bed.

∧⋏⋏

In his dream, the sky was impossibly blue, and the flowers were enormous, blossoms of pink, red, yellow, and orange, covering the landscape for miles around. After the flowers came groves of pine and aspen, and in the distance purple mountains towered over the scene. And then David remembered—he'd been here before.

Again he walked the gravel path, passing through the fields, the acres of bluebells. Everything seemed so peaceful, so beautiful, so *alive*. As he neared the forest, he noticed an elderly man sitting on a garden bench, reading from a large white book. As David approached, his grandfather looked up and smiled.

"David!" he said. "It's so good to see you again. But I'm afraid you owe me an apology."

"Why, Grandpa? What did I do?"

"You failed to remember."

Their previous conversation came flooding back to his mind.

"I did, didn't I."

"It's all right. You remember now, don't you."

David nodded. "You said I should look at the characters next to the circled one. And you said I shouldn't worry about what other people have said—that I should look at the characters for myself." He remembered the last session at the library. "That's what I decided too."

"Good; that's exactly right." His grandfather thumbed through the book, finally stopping at a page with big, bold letters. "Now here's an interesting page," he said. He showed the book to David.

The Book of Mormon
Another Testament of Jesus Christ

David smiled. "I have read it, you know."

"You've read the Book of Mormon, yes. But have you read the title page?"

"I usually start at 'I, Nephi,' I guess."

"Next time, start at the beginning. It's important."

"Okay." David nodded. "I will."

"Now," his grandfather said, "I have something I want to read to you." He turned back the pages. "'It came to pass, as they went, that he entered into a certain village: and a certain woman named Martha received him into her house. And she had a sister called Mary, which also sat at Jesus' feet, and heard his word. But Martha was cumbered about much serving, and came to him, and said, Lord, dost thou not care that my sister hath left me to serve alone? bid her therefore that she help me. And Jesus answered and said unto her, Martha, Martha, thou art careful and troubled about many things: but one thing is needful: and Mary hath chosen that good part.'" He looked intently at David. "Do you know what that one thing is?"

"Yes. And I've been trying, Grandpa."

"I know. That's why you're here. But you're careful and troubled about many things. Don't worry so much about all these philosophical matters. Look at what's right in front of you—really *look*. You'll see that the truth isn't so complicated. Just choose the good part."

"In spite of everything?"

"Yes. Having faith means we don't have all the answers. We can't figure everything out ahead of time." His grandfather smiled. "Remember the stairs? Go forward, as far as your light will shine. When you do, the light will move farther ahead through the darkness. Then you can move forward again. Just *don't stop*."

"All right. I'll keep going."

"Good."

David paused. "What if I forget again?"

His grandfather laughed. "Well, last time, you *were* clubbed in the head; it wasn't entirely your fault. But this time, I'll give you something—a token—to jog your memory." On his finger was a silver ring. He took it off, then handed it to David. "Wear this," he said. "It will remind you of me, and of the things we've talked about."

David put on the ring, which fit perfectly.

When he woke up, the sun was rising over the mountains.

JULY, 1835

Dear Brother:

. . . To give a minute rehearsal of a lengthy interview with a heavenly messenger, is very difficult, unless one is assisted immediately with the gift of inspiration. There is another item I wish to notice on the subject of visions. The Spirit you know, searches all things, even the deep things of God. When God manifests to his servants those things that are to come, or those which have been, he does it by unfolding them by the power of that Spirit which comprehends all things, always; and so much may be shown and made perfectly plain to the understanding in a short time, that to the world, who are occupied all their life to learn a little, look at the relation of it, and are disposed to call it false. You will understand then, by this, that while those glorious things were being rehearsed, the vision was also opened, so that our brother was permitted to see and understand much more full and perfect than I am able to communicate in writing. I know much may be conveyed to the understanding in writing, and many marvelous truths set forth with the pen, but after all it is but a shadow, compared to an open vision of seeing, hearing and realizing eternal things. . . .

. . . A remarkable fact is to be noticed with regard to this vision. In ancient time the Lord warned some of his servants in dreams: for instance, Joseph, the husband of Mary, was warned in a dream to take the young child and his mother, and flee into Egypt: also, the wise men were warned of the Lord in a dream not to return to Herod; and when "out of Egypt the Son was called," the angel of the Lord appeared in a dream to Joseph again: also he was warned in a dream to turn aside into the parts of Galilee. Such were the manifestations to Joseph, the favored descendant of the father of the faithful in dreams, and in them the Lord fulfilled his purposes: But the tone of which I have been speaking is what would have been called an open vision. And though it was in the night, yet it was not a dream. There is no room for conjecture in this matter, and to talk of deception would be to sport with the common sense of every man who knows when he is awake, when he sees and when he does not see. . . .

Oliver Cowdery

CHAPTER 38

A s David got ready for work that morning, he decided to spiff up a little more than usual—he wanted to look good when he went to see April. He put on his blue pinstripe suit and his maroon tie—a nice combination, he thought. Then he sorted through the box of old tie tacks that had belonged to his grandfather—the one his grandmother had given him after the funeral. One of the tie tacks featured an American flag—he remembered his grandfather wearing that one often. Another displayed a blue eyeball—his grandfather had sometimes worn that one for fun. Finally, he found the diamond tie tack he'd been looking for. But next to it, in the bottom of the box, was something he hadn't expected—a silver CTR ring. When had his grandfather worn that? He fished it out from the tie tacks, then put it on his finger. It fit perfectly. *Choose The Right,* he thought. And as he did so, he felt his mind open: *Choose the one good thing,* his grandfather had said. And he remembered everything—the beautiful gardens, the wrought-iron bench, the conversations with the old man who meant so much to him. And the ring! Had all of that been real? Or just figments of a dream? What was the truth?

But he was sick of that question; it never seemed to have an answer. And finally, he didn't care anymore. The ring was real, right there on his finger, literally a gift from beyond the grave. He was finished with doubt; he was going to do exactly what his grandfather had said—go forward with faith, trusting that the Church was true.

And with that thought, he felt what he could later describe only as a pinpoint of light, right in the center of his chest. As he watched it, paid attention to it, it began to expand, growing brighter and brighter, until it filled his heart, his mind, his whole being, with knowledge, with understanding, with certainty. There were no answers needing answers needing answers. As his grandfather had said, the truth wasn't so complicated; it was what it was. It brought its own witness, carried its own conviction.

He started to cry; then he started to laugh. *So this is what they mean,* he thought. He fell to his knees. "Thank you, Father in heaven," he prayed. "Thank you for answering my prayer. Thank you for showing me the truth."

He prayed for some time. Then he got up and sat quietly on the couch, savoring what he'd experienced, enjoying the clear morning light. Finally he opened his Book of Mormon and turned to the title page, reading through the beautiful words:

> . . . And also to the convincing of the Jew and Gentile that JESUS is the CHRIST, the ETERNAL God, manifesting himself unto all nations.

Not just to nations, David thought. *To those who ask in faith, with sincerity and real intent.* Then he read on:

> And now, if there are faults they are the mistakes of men; wherefore, condemn not the things of God, that ye may be found spotless at the judgment-seat of Christ.

And there was his answer—the true response to his father's question: *"If there are faults they are the mistakes of men."*

Nothing in this world is perfect, he realized. *And we don't have all the answers. But we can still know the truth.*

He looked at his watch—he needed to get to work. But suddenly, he knew he wasn't going to work; he was going to call in and take the day off. Then he was going to see April. He could hardly wait to tell her.

OCTOBER, 1834

𝕩 ≋ ⊣

Dear Brother,—

. . . The Lord, who is rich in mercy, and ever willing to answer the consistent prayer of the humble, after we had called upon him in a fervent manner, aside from the abodes of men, condescended to manifest to us his will. On a sudden, as from the midst of eternity, the voice of the Redeemer spake peace to us, while the vail was parted and the angel of God came down clothed with glory, and delivered the anxiously looked for message, and the keys of the gospel of repentance!—What joy! what wonder! what amazement! While the world were racked and distracted—while millions were groping as the blind for the wall, and while all men were resting upon uncertainty, as a general mass, our eyes beheld—our ears heard. As in the "blaze of day;" yes, more—above the glitter of the May Sun beam, which then shed its brilliancy over the face of nature! Then his voice, though mild, pierced to the center, and his words, "I am thy fellow-servant," dispelled every fear. We listened—we gazed—we admired! 'Twas the voice of the angel from glory—'twas a message from the Most High! and as we heard we rejoiced, while his love enkindled upon our souls, and we were rapt in the vision of the Almighty! Where was room for doubt? No where: uncertainty had fled, doubt had sunk, no more to rise, while fiction and deception had fled forever! . . .

Oliver Cowdery

CHAPTER 39

D avid practically ran through the lobby of the Church
Office Building, then hurried past the guard at the
library, who grabbed him by the sleeve and made him
sign in: "Whoa, there. ID, please. And name and time, right
here."

"Sorry," David said. "I'm in kind of a hurry." He signed
in, then pushed through the library door, looking for April.
But she didn't seem to be around. In fact, nobody seemed to
be around—except for Margaret, the older woman sorting
books in a room behind the counter. She came out to greet
him.

"Hello, David," she said. "You're looking for April, I suppose." She peered over the top of her glasses.

"Yes," he said. "Have you seen her?"

She started to laugh. "Actually, she went out looking for
you. She had a feeling you were on your way over."

"Thanks," David said. "Thanks a million."

He ran back through the doors, past the guard—who
made him sign out—and into the lobby. And there was April,
hurrying over the plush carpet toward him.

"David," she said. She put her hand on his arm. "I knew
you were coming. What's going on?"

"I prayed," he said. "I got my answer."

"Oh, David, that's wonderful!" She gave him a hug, then stood back and looked at him. "I knew it was something like that—I just knew it." She hugged him again.

"Listen," he said, "can we go somewhere and talk?"

"The plaza." She took his hand and pulled him toward the door.

"Don't you have to tell them you're going?"

She grinned. "I already did."

∧∧∧

That early in the day, the plaza was quiet—they had it all to themselves. So they sat at a table with a good view of the temple through the trees. Reaching over, April took his hand. "Where'd you get the CTR ring?"

He shook his head. "It's quite a story." He told her about his experience in the hospital, then about his dream the night before. And finally, he told her about the answer to his prayer, the witness he'd received that morning.

"It's really something, isn't it," she said.

"It sure is—but not what I expected."

"What did you expect?"

"Just a feeling of warmth and peace."

"But it was a lot more than that, wasn't it."

He nodded. "Yes, it was. Now I know, April. I really know."

She smiled, tilting her head. "Maybe now you'll be more enthusiastic about translating that transcript."

"Actually," he said, "I was hoping you might have time to help me look at it today."

"Did you bring your copy of the original?"

He pulled it out of his pocket. "Grandpa said to just look at it—to really *look* at it."

"All right. Let's look."

185

Together they stared at the photocopy.

They pored over it for several minutes, but nothing unusual happened. Finally, David felt a little foolish.

April looked over at him. "See anything?"

"Nothing in particular."

"Maybe it's too obvious."

"Okay," he said. "Let's talk about that. What's obvious?"

"Well," she said, "there are lots of strange characters."

"Right."

"In two separate sections—large and small."

"Right."

"Why two sections?"

He shrugged. "I don't know."

They looked at the paper a while longer, listening to the breeze in the trees, the sound of water from the reflecting pool.

"I don't think we're getting anywhere," he finally said.

"What else are we supposed to do?"

"He said to read the title page—although I did that this morning."

"Did you bring a Book of Mormon?"

"A Scout is prepared." Solemnly he saluted, then reached into his inner suit pocket, bringing out the old paperback.

"Looks like you need a new one," April said.

"I like this one—it has some history to it."

He opened the book to the title page, and the two started reading:

THE
BOOK OF MORMON

AN ACCOUNT WRITTEN BY

THE HAND OF MORMON

UPON PLATES
TAKEN FROM THE PLATES OF NEPHI

Wherefore, it is an abridgment of the record of the people of Nephi, and also of the Lamanites—Written to the Lamanites, who are a remnant of the house of Israel; and also to Jew and Gentile—Written by way of commandment, and also by the spirit of prophecy and of revelation—Written and sealed up, and hid up unto the Lord, that they might not be destroyed—To come forth by the gift and power of God unto the interpretation thereof—Sealed by the hand of Moroni, and hid up unto the Lord, to come forth in due time by way of the Gentile—The interpretation thereof by the gift of God.

An abridgment taken from the Book of Ether also, which is a record of the people of Jared, who were scattered at the time the Lord confounded the language of the people, when they were building a tower to get to heaven—Which is to show unto the remnant of the House of Israel what great things the Lord hath done for their fathers; and that they may know the covenants of the Lord, that they are not cast off forever—And also to the convincing of the Jew and Gentile that JESUS is the CHRIST, the ETERNAL God, manifesting himself unto all nations—And now, if there are faults they are the mistakes of men; wherefore, condemn not the things of God, that ye may be found spotless at the judgment-seat of Christ.

TRANSLATED BY JOSEPH SMITH, Jun.

"See anything obvious?" April said.

"The title."

"Right."

"Mormon wrote it."

"Right."

"Two paragraphs of explanation."

"Right."

Slowly it dawned on him.

"April," he said, "there are two paragraphs of explanation."

She started to smile. "There are, aren't there."

"There are *two paragraphs of explanation.*"

"And two sections of characters," she said.

"Two paragraphs of explanation!"

"And two sections of characters!" She threw her arms around his neck and kissed him. Then she quickly drew back, putting her hands up to her cheeks. "I'm sorry, I'm sorry. I was just so excited. I didn't mean—"

He took her hands. "It's all right," he said. "Really, it is." Then he kissed her back. He didn't think he'd ever been happier.

/\/\/\

At first, they couldn't see any correlation between the transcript and the two paragraphs on the Book of Mormon's title page. But there was still that pesky circled character they'd wondered so much about. "All right," David said. "What's so special about the circled character and its neighbors?" He brought out his grandfather's copy of the transcript.

April shook her head. "Nothing I can see."

He scanned the lines of small characters. "Look," he said, pointing. "The two characters in front of the circled one are repeated at the start of the last line."

"Interesting." She paused. "The character *after* the circled one is repeated next."

He looked up. "Are there any repeated words or phrases on the title page—toward the bottom?"

"Good question." She pulled the open book in front of them.

"The pattern we're looking for goes something like this." He pulled out a pencil and wrote in the margin.

[word 1] [word 2] [unique word] [word 3]
[word 1] [word 2] [word 3]

"Right."

"And remember—this is a translation, so it might not be exact."

"Okay."

"And look for main words—articles and prepositions may not count."

For several minutes, they scanned through the words and phrases, looking for any kind of repetition.

"I'm not seeing any," April said. "There are repeated words, but not in that pattern."

"Right." He paused, thinking. "How about in the first paragraph?"

"Why would they be in the first paragraph?"

"I don't know. Sometimes you just have to try things." He winked.

"Point taken."

After a few minutes of scanning, April said, "I see that pattern—but it's not in the right place to match the transcript."

"Maybe that's okay," he said. "What are you looking at?"

"'The gift and power of God,' six lines down, and 'the gift of God,' at the end of the paragraph."

"Wow," he said. "If that's right, then the circled character means 'power.'"

"Do you think that's it?"

"I don't know. But it might give us something to start with."

"But it's in the wrong paragraph. And on the transcript, it's not at the end of the paragraph."

"True. But we don't know how Joseph copied the paragraphs, or in what order they originally came in. At the time, he probably couldn't even read them."

She smiled. "I think you're stretching."

"Maybe so. But I'm going to keep after it. 'Don't stop,' Grandpa said."

She took his hand. "That's very good advice."

CHAPTER 40

For Thornton, just being in the courtroom was depressing enough, watching the pathetic parade of drug dealers, petty thieves, and wife beaters appearing before the judge. Worse, however, was being part of the parade—handcuffed, shackled, and wearing an orange jumpsuit, sitting in the "peanut gallery" with the rest of the prisoners.

As he looked out over the courtroom, he noticed David Hunter sitting toward the front, but he was surprised to see Tamara—dressed to the nines—sitting next to him. He smiled at her. She'd been crying, but she managed a small wave—for Thornton, a good sign.

Finally, the clerk called Thornton's name, and he shuffled to the bench with his state-appointed attorney. The judge did not look friendly, nor did he appear to be in a good mood. He consulted his papers, then looked up at Thornton.

"Thornton Price," he said, "you have been charged with six counts of felony theft and one count of conspiring to blackmail. How do you plead?"

Thornton looked at his attorney, then back at the judge. "Guilty, your honor."

"You understand that you have the right to a trial?"

"Yes, your honor."

"And you are voluntarily waiving that right?"

"Yes, sir."

"Very well." The judge leaned back in his chair. "Mr. Price, I have reviewed the facts of this case very carefully, including a statement made in your behalf by Agent David Hunter of the FBI. I understand you were coerced into the conspiracy—you were blackmailed yourself."

"It's my own fault, your honor."

"Yes, it is—and I want you to keep that in mind. Nevertheless, I believe that your participation is mitigated by several factors: First, you have no previous record. Second, you saved Agent Hunter's life—by hitting him in the head, ironically enough, but really by having the decency to keep him hidden from the other conspirators. Third, after he was shot, you phoned for help and provided first aid until professional care could arrive. Finally, you identified the other conspirators and turned yourself in. For those reasons, I will not be imposing a sentence for conspiracy."

"Thank you, your honor."

The judge leaned forward, clasping his hands. "But I hope you have learned, Mr. Price, that crime does not pay; it only leads to deeper problems—I see them every day. The truth is, you and your wife could easily have been killed, and I doubt that your employer will continue to need your services."

Thornton nodded.

"Now, I have not imposed a sentence for conspiracy. The counts of theft, however, are a different matter. I sentence you to two months in the county jail for each count—twelve months in all. You will also make monetary restitution to the LDS Church for the documents you stole. In addition, you will be placed on supervised probation for one year after your release from prison. Do you understand?"

"Yes, your honor."

"Very well." The judge banged his gavel on the desk. "Next case."

⋀⋀⋀

Later that day, Thornton was thrilled to learn that he had a visitor—Tamara had come to see him, looking as beautiful as ever. Watching her through the glass window, he wished he could touch her face, hold her hand. But all he could do was talk through the barrier.

"Hello, darling. Thank you for being in court today. It meant a lot."

"Thornton, I just hate seeing you in here."

"I deserve it."

"Maybe so. But I've been thinking a lot since our last visit, and you were right—this is partly my fault."

He shook his head. "Not really. You asked if I couldn't have made money honestly. I should have found a way."

"Yes, you should. But I pressured you. I've been too concerned about appearances. That's something I'm going to change."

Thornton felt hope rising inside him. "Does this mean you'll stay with me?"

She wiped her eyes. "No, it doesn't. I'm still very upset about all this. But I do understand what happened now; you saved that agent's life."

"I nearly got him killed."

"I know. But in the end, you learned who you really are. That's something, at least."

For a moment, Thornton couldn't speak. Finally he said, "You've always believed in me. Even now, you still do."

She nodded. "That doesn't mean I forgive you."

"I know." He choked up again. "Where will you go?"

"I'll be staying with my parents, at least for a while."

"And after that?"

She sighed. "I don't know. We'll have to see."

"Will you at least visit me again?"

"I don't think so. I hate it here, Thornton, and this place is just so—so—"

Thornton felt a flare of anger. "What? So low-class? I thought you were going to stop caring so much about appearances."

"Okay," she said. "You're right. But I'm having a hard time dealing with all this. Right now I'm just so mad—at both of us, really. We've been so shallow, so stupid. Maybe we're just wrong for each other."

"Don't say that," he said. "Please. Let's try to work things out."

At first she didn't say anything. Then she choked out, "I'll come again next week; I can't promise anything more than that."

"Thank you," he said. And he knew, for now, that was really all he could ask.

CHAPTER 41

S eth Pitt flexed his shoulders, then swung the ax, splitting the large section of log right down the middle. He enjoyed the sensation, the *whack* of the blade as it bit the wood, the smell of the pine, the clunk of the pieces as they struck the ground. After he finished, he piled the wood into the shed in his mother's backyard, thinking of the warmth it would give her several months later when winter arrived. He'd actually done quite a few things around the place—repaired the tears in the screen door, plugged a hole in the roof, replaced light bulbs, fixed leaky faucets. He knew that his mother was wondering what had gotten into him, but he wouldn't reveal anything. "You told me I needed to do some chores," he'd say.

He'd also made efforts to change his appearance, shaving his head and growing a mustache, and he wouldn't go out without sunglasses and an old baseball cap, and then not for long.

But today, he did need to go out. Closing and fastening the shed door, he pulled down the brim of his cap, walked over to Main Street, and caught bus 37, which he rode to a pawn shop on 35th South.

A bell on the door jingled as he walked inside, and the

man behind the counter greeted him. "Help you find anything?"

"Just looking."

The man nodded, and Seth wandered over to a display case full of jewelry—old wedding rings, brooches, and other items. A lot of it looked like junk, but an elegant gold chain with a ruby pendant caught his eye. "How much for the necklace?" he asked.

The man came over to the counter. "Well," he said, "that's the real deal—solid gold and genuine rubies. It's a beauty, isn't it?"

Seth nodded.

"I think we could let that go for around eight hundred dollars."

"I can give you four hundred."

The man shook his head. "Got nearly that much in it. Give me seven hundred, and we'll call it a deal."

"Sorry," Seth said. "Maybe some other time."

"Need something for your girlfriend?"

"My mother."

"Well, in that case, I'd like to help you out. Let's say six hundred."

"Like I said—four hundred is all I've got."

"Sorry. Can't do it for that."

"All right," Seth said. "I understand."

"Is there anything else you need?"

Seth looked around the store.

"Well, I could use some ammunition—.40 caliber."

"Now, *that* we've got in your price range."

CHAPTER 42

꒦꒷꒕ L

David woke up with a start. He'd been dreaming about the Book of Mormon again, but even in his dream, he'd had a realization. He reached for the pencil and pad of paper he kept on his nightstand, then wrote out his thoughts as a sort of syllogism:

A. The Book of Mormon is true.

B. Therefore Joseph Smith translated it from the gold plates.

C. Therefore the coded Joseph Smith letter is false.

But the letter wasn't false. It had been authenticated by the experts, at least as far as anything could be authenticated.

He crossed out item C and wrote in a new one:

C. Therefore something else is going on with the coded Joseph Smith letter.

And then he realized—he had to see the letter itself, not just a photocopy. "There's nothing like seeing the real thing," April had said. And with her connections, she was just the person to help him do it.

∧∧∧

Wearing the mandatory white gloves, David held the coded Joseph Smith letter up to the light. Several members of the University of Utah's library staff were looking on, including Stephanie Carlson, the head of Special Collections. David felt a little odd handling this scrap of paper that had caused him so much trouble. The letter was in poor condition, with ragged edges, faded ink, and a dark brown stain at the bottom. He was no expert, but the letter certainly looked authentic, and the experts had said it was. It was the stain that was bothering him.

"May I ask a stupid question?" he asked.

"Sure—my favorite kind," Stephanie said.

"Would it be possible to remove this stain—scrape it off or something?"

She laughed. "I wouldn't even try—that letter is far too important. If we were to damage it . . . Well, you understand. Conserving documents is kind of like practicing medicine: 'First, do no harm.'"

"That's what I figured." David paused, thinking. "Is there any way to see if there's writing under the stain?"

Stephanie looked around at the other librarians. "*Under* the stain? Now that's an interesting idea. It might be possible."

"How would you do it?"

"Multispectral imaging. We take pictures of a document using different ranges of the spectrum, and then we put them together in different combinations. When we hit the right one, the result is pretty amazing. We can do it here, but the real experts are at BYU."

"No kidding?"

"Oh, yes. Really, BYU is at the vanguard of that technology—among the best in the world."

David looked to see if she was pulling his leg, but she

seemed perfectly serious, and the others in the room were nodding in agreement.

She cleared her throat. "For example," she continued, "BYU is working with Oxford University on ancient documents from Oxyrhynchus, and they're reading Greek and Latin scrolls that were carbonized during the eruption of Mount Vesuvius. The documents are completely black, but they can read them."

"Wow. But you've never done that with this letter?"

"No. We weren't looking for more text; we were just trying to determine if the letter was authentic. That's what we tested."

"Could we check? Could we try that multi . . . whatever it is?" David smiled.

"Multispectral imaging. Sure."

"When could we do it?"

"How about now?"

.ᴧʌᴧ

David watched with amazement as John Shafer, from the university's engineering department, showed him how the multispectral imager worked. Using a test document written with two kinds of ink, he changed the part of the spectrum by which the document was viewed. At first, David didn't see anything different. But as John continued to change the light wavelength, gradually the writing in one kind of ink faded out, while the writing in the other kind became darker, easier to read.

David smiled. "Sort of a Urim and Thummim."

"Well, yes." John smiled wryly. "If you believe that sort of thing." He removed the test document. "Now let's try the Joseph Smith letter." Carefully, he mounted it in the machine, then began moving through the various frequencies of the spectrum. As David watched, the stain darkened in color.

"Wrong way," John said, smiling. He turned the dials. As he did so, this time the ink darkened, and the stain began to lighten, then disappear. As it did, where the stain had been, new characters began to appear, faint at first, then becoming darker and darker.

"Look at that!" John said. "You were right—there's more writing under the stain. It's a postscript from Joseph Smith—in code."

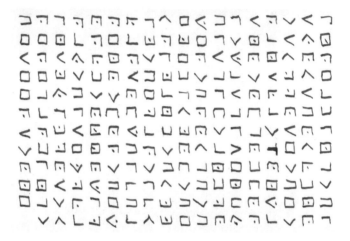

David could hardly believe it. He'd been hopeful, yes. But something like this . . . "Can we take a picture of that?" he asked excitedly.

"Don't worry," John said. "We'll be taking plenty."

CHAPTER 43

That night, at home, David started translating the hidden section of pigpen code, being careful to read it sideways, unlike the first section that had given him so much trouble. This time, knowing the secret, he found that deciphering the message was easy. In addition, he had most of the key memorized by now, although he still had to refer to it for a few of the characters.

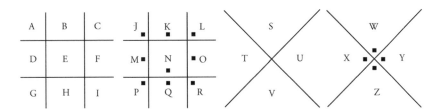

As he worked, he wrote the deciphered text on a new sheet of paper.

inreadingthisyoushouldnotsupposethetranslationwasnot ofGodforitwasgivenbyhisgiftandpowerthroughthemediu moftheurimandthummimtheparticularsofwhicharenotforthe worldtoknowipraythisexplainsmyimpostureregardingthe seerstone

When he finished, he rewrote the text with spacing and punctuation, making it easier to read.

> In reading this, you should not suppose the translation was not of God, for it was given by His gift and power through the medium of the Urim and Thummim, the particulars of which are not for the world to know. I pray this explains my imposture regarding the seerstone.

The result was thrilling. He shot both arms above his head in a gesture of triumph. The last part of the message showed that Joseph Smith *had* translated the Book of Mormon from the gold plates, just as he'd always said. But in that case, what did the *first* part of the message mean? David shook his head. Just as he'd thought he understood what was going on, a new mystery was beginning to emerge.

The next morning, news about the hidden portion of the letter was all over the television. Like David, several other people had decoded the rest of the characters, and how to do that was fairly well known by now. One of the news programs featured a story about local grade-school kids who were using the code to pass messages back and forth in class. "It's fun!" one little girl said. "We can send notes to each other, and the other kids can't read them."

The interviewer looked puzzled. "You and your friends are the only ones who know the code?"

"Well, at first. Now quite a few of the kids know."

"How about your teacher?"

The girl looked sheepish. "At first we didn't think so. But then we found out she did."

"Did you get in trouble?"

"Just a little. We were passing notes about a boy we liked." The girl giggled.

/\/\/\

David was at work, starting on a new case, when his phone rang. He picked it up but didn't recognize the voice.

"Brother Hunter?"

"Yes?"

"This is Mary Frazier from the Church's Public Relations office. Some of the Brethren will be holding a press conference this afternoon—3:00 at the Joseph Smith Memorial Building. They'd like you to attend, if you can."

David smiled. "Do I have to wear a suit?"

"That would be appropriate, yes."

"I know," he said, now embarrassed. "I was kidding. My suit and I will be there. Thanks for the invitation."

/\/\/\

David arrived early at the Joseph Smith Memorial Building, where he watched as the news crews set up cameras and microphones in the luxurious lobby, and a crew of Church employees brought in chairs and a podium. Then other people began coming in through the front doors, eventually filling the room. David recognized some of them as government and business leaders; others seemed to be Church employees and maybe even people off the street. Finally, the First Presidency came in from the east hallway, accompanied by several members of the Twelve. They shook hands with David, who was a bit awestruck to be so close to these men whom he'd seen before only on television.

"We'd like to thank you for what you've done," President Iverson said, pumping David's hand. "The Church would have kept moving forward anyway, but it's nice to know the rest of the story, so to speak."

"I'm glad I was able to help," David said. "It's wonderful that the Prophet has been vindicated."

"You have a testimony, don't you, young man."

"Yes, sir, I do." David was thrilled to be able to say that.

"I could tell," the president said. He gave David a wink, then waved his hand toward the chairs. "We'd like you to sit behind the podium with us, if you don't mind."

"Are you sure?"

The president simply smiled.

"It would be an honor, sir," David said.

President Iverson stepped to the podium and called the conference to order. "Thank you for coming," he said. "In our previous news conference, I said of the Joseph Smith letter, 'There's more to this than meets the eye. We haven't seen the end of this.' He paused. "At the time, I had no idea how literally true that would turn out to be."

The crowd laughed.

"Now we know that there *is* more to the letter, thanks to FBI agent David Hunter, whom I would like to thank and congratulate. We are happy to have him with us here today."

The camera moved to David, then back to President Iverson.

"I'd like to tell you a story from the early days of the Church. In 1839 Joseph Smith, Sidney Rigdon, and others traveled to Washington, D.C., to present petitions for redress for crimes against the Church in Missouri. During the trip, they were invited to speak to a crowd of three thousand people in Philadelphia. Sidney Rigdon addressed the group first. Wanting to avoid confrontation, he used the Bible to show that the Church was true, avoiding any reference to the revelations of the Restoration. The Prophet was visibly disappointed; Parley P. Pratt observed that he could barely sit still.

"Elder Pratt wrote, 'When Sidney Rigdon was through,

brother Joseph arose like a lion about to roar; and being full of the Holy Ghost, spoke in great power, bearing testimony of the visions he had seen, the ministering of angels which he had enjoyed; and how he had found the plates of the Book of Mormon, and translated them by the gift and power of God. He commenced by saying: "If nobody else had the courage to testify of so glorious a record, he felt to do it in justice to the people, and leave the event to God." The entire congregation was astounded; electrified, as it were, and overwhelmed with the sense of truth and power by which he spoke, and the wonders which he related. A lasting impression was made; many souls were gathered into the fold. And I bear witness, that he, by his faithful and powerful testimony, cleared his garments of their blood.'

"Now," the president said, "many of you have remained similarly steadfast in your testimonies. You have defended the Book of Mormon in the face of ridicule and doubt. You have continued to bear witness of the Prophet Joseph and the glorious truths he taught, even when all looked dark. Upon you I leave my blessing, my gratitude, and my love.

"I would like to conclude with a few of the Prophet's words that seem particularly appropriate in light of recent events. He said of this great latter-day work, 'The Standard of Truth has been erected; no unhallowed hand can stop the work from progressing; persecutions may rage, mobs may combine, armies may assemble, calumny may defame, but the truth of God will go forth boldly, nobly, and independent, till it has penetrated every continent, visited every clime, swept every country, and sounded in every ear, till the purposes of God shall be accomplished, and the Great Jehovah shall say the work is done.'

"That this is true, I bear my humble witness. May God bless you all."

CHAPTER 44

Receptionist Beth Wilkerson punched a button, then picked up the receiver. "Federal Bureau of Investigation," she said crisply.

"Good afternoon," the caller said. "Is David Hunter available?"

"I'm sorry, but Agent Hunter is out on assignment."

"Do you know when he might be back?"

"I'm afraid I can't give out that information."

"All right; I understand. What time do you close there?"

"The main office closes at five."

"Thanks," the man said. "Maybe I can get him after work."

"I'd be glad to make an appointment for you," she said. "He should be available in the morning." But the man had hung up.

That's odd, she thought. She turned back to her typewriter. She was better with the computer, but the FBI still used a few paper forms, and she had 112 of them that had to be filled out before the day was over.

David was tired, and a little rattled. He'd been out on a dangerous assignment—an abduction perpetrated by a man from Colorado. A previous sex offender, the man had kid-napped a fourteen-year-old neighbor girl and transported her to Salt Lake City, then holed up with a gun in a hotel near the airport. David had been part of the team involved in tracking him down and talking him out of the hotel. The negotiator had done a good job, and no one had gotten hurt, but the possibility had certainly been there.

Now David was walking from the parking lot to the back door of the FBI offices, glad to call it a day. To his shock, he heard the *whang* of a gunshot—close, too—and saw the bullet strike the wall of the building in front of him, propelling a chunk of brick into the stratosphere. He grabbed his gun and turned, trying to squeeze off a shot, but it was too late—the shooter had fired again, this time more accurately, and David went down onto the asphalt, breathless with terror, his senses sharpened to absolute clarity. Strangely, he couldn't move, so he lay face up, noticing the cotton clouds in the blue, blue sky, the sparrows quarreling on the power lines overhead. How odd that everything seemed so normal, when, in his chest, the pain was growing sharper with every labored breath. He gri-maced, then managed to turn his head just as the shooter came around the row of cars. It was Seth Pitt, and his pistol was aimed straight at David's head.

"Well, Agent Hunter," he said, "now you know how it feels."

David groaned. "What are you talking about?"

"You killed Sonny."

"You're crazy." David shut his eyes, trying not to panic. "*You're* the one who killed Sonny."

"You *shut up*!" Seth shouted. "If you hadn't been there, Sonny would still be alive. The bullet that killed him was meant for you. Now I've finished the job."

David coughed, then glanced over at his gun, which had spun several feet away on the asphalt.

"Don't even think about it," Seth said. "I wouldn't want to blow your head off, too. I'd like you to look nice for your funeral." He started to laugh.

But then another shot cut him off, hitting him in the shoulder, followed by one more to the chest. Seth staggered, then crumpled heavily to the ground. For a moment his body shuddered, but he finally lay still, the deep-red blood pooling under his back, his blank eyes staring into space.

Agent Wilcox knelt by the body, retrieving the gun and making sure the man was really dead. Then he strode over to David. "Are you okay?" he said. "Can you get up?"

"Maybe if you help me." Wilcox grabbed David's wrists, pulling him to his feet in one quick motion, then supported him while he got his balance.

Standing on his own, David was still shaken—and sore. "Even with a bulletproof vest," he said, "getting hit in the chest hurts like crazy."

"You'll probably have a nice, big bruise to show for it." Wilcox smiled grimly, then looked down at Seth. "What a wasted life."

The two men studied the silent form. He wouldn't be any more trouble—aside from their having to clean up the mess.

Wilcox stuffed his hands into his pockets. "I want you to practice your shooting, Hunter. Next time, you could be on your own."

"I'll never be as good as you."

"Well, that goes without saying." Wilcox paused. "Sorry," he said. "I don't mean to joke. I never like having to kill someone."

"Thanks for being there," David said. "That was close."

"It's a good thing I came in behind you. If I'd been a little earlier, he might have shot us both. A little later, well . . ." He looked down. "He was a bad man."

"Yes, he was. I'm not sorry he's dead."

"Neither am I. Unfortunately, there's always another one where he came from."

David shook his head. "I know."

JULY, 1835

꩜ ≋ ꜠

Dear Brother:

. . . This vale [near the Hill Cumorah, after the last great battle between the Nephites and Lamanites,] was destined to consume the fair forms and vigorous systems of tens of thousands of the human race—blood mixed with blood, flesh with flesh, bones with bones, and dust with dust! When the vital spark which animated their clay had fled, each lifeless lump lay on one common level—cold and inanimate. Those bosoms which had burned with rage against each other for real or supposed injury, had now ceased to heave with malice; those arms which were, a few moments before nerved with strength, had alike become paralyzed, and those hearts which had been fired with revenge, had now ceased to beat, and the head to think— in silence, in solitude, and in disgrace alike, they have long since turned to earth, to their mother dust, to await the august, and to millions, awful hour, when the trump of the Son of God shall echo and re-echo from the skies, and they come forth, quickened and immortalized, to not only stand in each other's presence, but before the bar of him who is Eternal! . . .

Oliver Cowdery

CHAPTER 45

ᢖᡬ ≋ ᠴᡨᠨ

B
ack at home, David gathered up all of his notes about the coded Joseph Smith letter, then went to his computer and typed in the complete text of the document—the first time he'd seen the whole thing in one piece:

Dear Brother:

It is with sensations of regret that I write these few lines in relation to the Book of Mormon. I cannot any longer forbear throwing off the mask, and letting you know the secret.

I have practised a deception in pretending to translate the Book of Mormon through the medium of a seerstone, which never was the case. This you have long suspected, together with the conniving between the Witnesses and myself in relation to this matter.

I omit other important things which could I see you I could make you acquainted with.

Farewell untill I return,

Joseph Smith Jr.

P.S.

In reading this, you should not suppose the translation was not of God, for it was given by his gift and power through the medium of the Urim and Thummim, the particulars of which are not for the world to know. I pray this explains my imposture regarding the seerstone.

J.S.

So it wasn't that Joseph had "practised a deception in pretending to translate the Book of Mormon." It was that he had "practised a deception in pretending to translate the Book of Mormon *through the medium of a seerstone*"—quite a different thing.

Evidently, the Prophet and his associates had made up an alternate story of how the plates were translated. David knew from his research that people in the early 1800s sometimes used seerstones to find lost objects and look for buried treasure. Had the stones really worked? David thought it unlikely, although he could understand why people of the time might believe such an explanation for the translation. But why would it be necessary?

He rifled through his papers, again reading David Whitmer's description of the process: "Joseph Smith would put the seer stone into a hat, and put his face in the hat, drawing it closely around his face to exclude the light; and in the darkness the spiritual light would shine. A piece of something resembling parchment would appear, and on that appeared the writing. One character at a time would appear, and under it was the interpretation in English. Brother Joseph would read off the English to Oliver Cowdery, who was his principal scribe, and when it was written down and repeated to Brother Joseph to see if it was correct, then it would disappear, and another character with the interpretation would appear. Thus the Book of Mormon was translated by the gift and power of God, and not by any power of man."

The Martin Harris account was essentially the same: "By aid of the seer stone, sentences would appear and were read by the prophet and written by Martin, and when finished he would say, 'written' and if correctly written, that sentence would disappear and another appear in its place, but if not written correctly it remained until corrected, so that the translation was just as it was engraved on the plates, precisely in the language then used."

But Oliver Cowdery—well, that was a different story. Late in his life, after his excommunication and then his return to the Church, he had addressed the Saints, saying, "I wrote with my own pen, the entire Book of Mormon (save a few pages), as it fell from the lips of the Prophet Joseph Smith, as he translated it by the gift and power of God, by the means of the Urim and Thummim, or, as it is called by that book, 'holy interpreters.' I beheld with my eyes and handled with my hands the gold plates from which it was translated. I also saw with my eyes and handled with my hands the 'holy interpreters.'"

Most interesting of all was what Joseph Smith had said at a Church conference in 1831, where his brother Hyrum had invited the Prophet to explain more fully to the Elders how the Book of Mormon came forth. Joseph responded that "it was not intended to tell the world all the particulars of the coming forth of the Book of Mormon; and also said that it was not expedient for him to relate these things."

Now David understood: The process was sacred, not for the world to know. Somehow, the Urim and Thummim, not the seerstone, had been used. But Joseph and Oliver didn't want others to know exactly how—which explained the alternate story.

David wished he understood how the translation had taken place. He imagined Joseph and Oliver, sitting at a handmade table, with the Prophet wearing the breastplate and the "interpreters," reading the Book of Mormon text to his scribe. "These were days never to be forgotten," Oliver had written later. "To sit under the sound of a voice dictated by the inspiration of heaven, awakened the utmost gratitude of this bosom! Day after day I continued, uninterrupted, to write from his mouth, as he translated with the Urim and Thummim, or, as the Nephites would have said, 'Interpreters,' the history or record called 'The Book of Mormon.'"

David would have given anything to be there.

CHAPTER 46

꒷ ≋ ⼧ ⊐

Each night after work, David continued working out the translation of the Book of Mormon characters his grandfather had left him—the Moroni Code. The breakthrough had been his and April's discovery that the circled character might mean "power," which had turned out to be the case. Some of its "neighbors," as his grandfather had called them, meant "gift" and "God," and by comparing these and other characters with words and phrases on the Book of Mormon's title page, he'd been able to work out even more of the text. To his surprise, it had turned out *not* to be the Title Page—at least David didn't think it was, although parts of it were close. He suspected that the transcript represented part of the Book of Mormon that had been lost by Martin Harris. If that was true, then he was reading writings of Mormon and Moroni that hadn't been understood since Joseph Smith translated them more than 150 years earlier. The thought gave him chills.

As far as he was able, David had written the literal translation of each line, followed by a cleaned-up version in standard English.

ACCOUNT ABRIDGED PRESERVEDrecordrecord ofMORMON
An account abridged from two records preserved by Mormon
SACREDENGRAVINGS PLATEStoPLATES CHRISTcausedtobeTAKENFROM
Sacred engravings, transcribed at the direction of Christ

He still had a long way to go, and figuring everything out would take time, but he was confident he could succeed. He smiled wryly as he recalled the Lord's words to Oliver Cowdery: "Behold, you have not understood; you have supposed that I would give it unto you, when you took no thought save it was to ask me. But, behold, I say unto you, that you must study it out in your mind."

Now that, David thought, *is an understatement.* He considered his life, everything that had happened since his grandmother had given him the faded slip of paper. He'd learned so much since that day. *The Lord will show us the way,* he thought, *but we still have to walk it.* It was a lesson he would never forget.

⋀⋀⋀

On Friday, David decided to go see April during her lunch hour—he had a special outing in mind for the next day. As he walked to the Church Office Building, he decided to go through Temple Square, where he could enjoy the shade of the giant chestnut trees, the smell of the flowers.

He stopped again to admire the temple, to marvel at the strength and solidity of the granite walls. He thought of Brigham Young, who had planned for this sacred edifice to last into the Millennium. Finally, he looked up at his old friend, the Big Dipper, but with different thoughts than last time. Yes, from a different planet, a different viewpoint, that pattern of stars wouldn't exist, wouldn't mean a thing. But he wasn't on a different planet; he was right here on good old planet Earth, and he was planning to stay a while—into the eternities, in fact. And that meant the pattern wasn't going to change—the constellation would be there for a long, long time, pointing the way back home.

OCTOBER, 1834

Dear Brother—

. . . Another day has passed, into that, to us, boundless ocean, *ETERNITY!* where nearly six thousand years have gone before; and what flits across the mind like an electric shock is, that it will never return! Whether it has been well improved or not; whether the principles emanated from *HIM* who "hallowed" it, have been observed; or whether, like the common mass of time, it has been heedlessly spent, is not for me to say—one thing I can say—It can never be recalled!—it has rolled in to assist in filling up the grand space decreed in the mind of its Author, till nature shall have ceased her work, and *time* its accustomed revolutions—when its Lord shall have completed the gathering of his elect, and with them enjoy that Sabbath which shall never end! . . .

I must close for the present: my candle is quite extinguished, and all nature seems locked in silence, shrouded in darkness, and enjoying that repose so necessary to this life. But the period is rolling on when night will close, and those who are found worthy will inherit that city where neither the light of the sun nor moon will be necessary! "For the glory of God will lighten it, and the Lamb will be the light thereof." . . .

O. Cowdery

EPILOGUE

T he next day, Saturday, David and April drove to his grandmother's house in Midvale. David knocked on the front door to let his grandmother know someone was there; then they walked inside. Things hadn't changed much since the funeral, and the living room always brought back vivid memories. And right now, the aroma from the kitchen was really something.

"Oh, David," his grandmother said, dusting her hands as she walked from the kitchen. "I was just making cookies. If you'll stay a few minutes, you can have some, hot out of the oven."

"That sounds great," he said.

"And who's this?"

"Grandma, I'd like you to meet someone who means a lot to me. This is April McKenzie."

"Hello, dear. I'm so pleased to meet you. I've been after David for years now to find a nice girl and settle down." She stood back, looking April over. "David, I think she might do quite nicely." Then she laughed.

"Grandma, you can really be embarrassing, you know that?"

"I do try," she said, laughing again. She patted April's

hand. "Don't mind me, dear. I'm just an old woman who loves her grandson."

"It's all right," April said. "I think quite a lot of him myself."

They all sat down and talked for a while. Then David's grandmother brought in cookies and glasses of milk. As they were eating, David had one more thing he wanted to talk about.

"Grandma, I'm here to make my report."

"Your report?"

"You gave me an assignment after Grandpa's funeral, remember?"

"Oh, *that* report. Well, it's about time. Go ahead; I'm all ears."

But suddenly David found himself unable to speak. Finally, he said, "I found out, Grandma. I finally know for myself."

"Oh, David, that's wonderful!" She wiped away a tear. "I knew you could do it."

He came over and put his arms around her frail shoulders. "And I learned one more thing, too."

"What's that?"

"We *will* see Grandpa again." Then he whispered, "I already did. We had a nice visit."

She pressed her cheek against his. "That's what I hear."

THE END

NOTES FOR THE CURIOUS

ᗡᖶ ≋ ᖶᕇ

Warning! Plot spoilers ahead! Don't read these notes until *after* you've read the novel.

At the beginning of this book, I said that with one exception, all of the quotations, documents, and artifacts mentioned in this book are real. The exception is the coded Joseph Smith letter, which is a figment of my imagination, although I created a fake version of the letter so a "photograph" of it could be included in the novel. Part of its wording is based on letters from the Prophet to Sidney Rigdon and Emma Smith on unrelated matters. (See *The Personal Writings of Joseph Smith*, rev. ed., edited by Dean C. Jessee [Salt Lake City: Deseret Book, 2002], 266–68, 580–82.)

It is true, however, that several of the early Brethren did sometimes write in pigpen code, and that on at least one occasion the Church obtained help from the FBI to decode a journal entry.

From this point in these notes, I'll include a passage from this book, followed by commentary. Here's the first one:

> *Page 2:* The next day, he put the plates into the box, resting them on the pillars. Near them he laid the other remaining treasures of his people, including the precious Interpreters. Finally, he pushed the large, rounded stone until

it completely covered the box, burying its contents in darkness, waiting for another prophet, another time.

For a detailed discussion of this, see appendix A, "The Stone Box."

> *Page 24:* That night, Joseph turned to his unfailing source of help. "Dear God," he prayed, "we are reduced in property, and my wife's father is about to turn us out of doors, and we have not where to go."

This and a few other bits of Joseph Smith's dialogue are real, taken from various historical sources. All of the writings from Oliver Cowdery are authentic, taken from letters written to William W. Phelps for inclusion in the *Messenger and Advocate,* the early Church's newspaper (October–December 1834; February, April, July, October 1835; all are included in Oliver Cowdery, *The Prophet and the Plates* [Salt Lake City: Temple Hill Books, 2007], available from Amazon.com). The revelations quoted are from the early sections of the Doctrine and Covenants, specifically sections 5, 6, 8, and 9.

> *Pages 26–27:* It was, in fact, the infamous forger Mark Hofmann's first important "discovery."

Mark William Hofmann, a disaffected member of The Church of Jesus Christ of Latter-day Saints, was a prolific forger and counterfeiter who murdered two people in Salt Lake City during the 1980s in an effort to hide his crimes. For more information (this and other Web sites were verified to be active and correct addresses as of July 11, 2007):

http://en.wikipedia.org/wiki/Mark_Hofmann.

Dallin H. Oaks, "Recent Events Involving Church History and Forged Documents," *Ensign,* October 1987, 63.

> *Page 34:* "Look, here's another one," April said. She was pointing at an extremely odd character in a copy of *Egyptian*

Grammar, by A. H. Gardiner. To David's surprise, it matched perfectly with a character from the first line of the transcript. They had now matched nearly thirty of the transcript characters with hieroglyphs from the Egyptian dictionary—many more than they had anticipated—and not just *simple* characters, either. Many of the symbols were unusual and complex.

See Ariel Crowley, "The Anthon Transcript," *Improvement Era,* January–March 1942, which is available online here:

http://www.shieldsresearch.org/Scriptures/BoM/
Anthon_Transcript-Crowley/Anthon_Transcript-Crowley.htm

Brother Crowley presents a whole series of characters from the Anthon Transcript matched with their Egyptian counterparts, noting, "The most difficult, complex characters appearing in the Anthon Transcript have been deliberately singled out [for comparison]." To advance the plot of this novel, I've included the idea that the Book of Mormon characters could match various symbol sets and, to a limited degree, that's true. However, to my admittedly untrained eye, Brother Crowley's numerous comparisons are most impressive. I've included only a few of them in this book.

More recent scholarship on the Anthon Transcript includes:

David E. Sloan, "The Anthon Transcripts and the Translation of the Book of Mormon: Studying It Out in the Mind of Joseph Smith," *Journal of Book of Mormon Studies* 5/2 (1996), 57–81. (Thanks to Jay Parry for identifying this article.) Also available at:

http://farms.byu.edu/display.php?table=jbms&id=124

Stanley B. Kimball, "The Anthon Transcript: People, Primary Sources, and Problems," *BYU Studies,* Spring 1970, 325–52. Also available at:

http://www.shieldsresearch.org/Scriptures/BoM/
BYUSAntn.html

Page 53: Several weeks had passed since David had last spoken with April, and the case of the stolen documents was being handled by the police, with no need for the FBI to get involved. So David was surprised when the Special Agent in Charge, Ted Wilcox, called him into his office on a Monday morning to talk about recent events at the Church Office Building.

On occasion, the Church has asked the FBI for assistance. For example, on October 20, 1985, the *Salt Lake Tribune* noted, "Speculation that the controversial 1830 Mormon 'white salamander' letter . . . is a forgery has prompted the church to send that letter to the Federal Bureau of Investigation's laboratory for authentication. Some of the voluminous documents found in both Mr. Hofmann's home and his burned-out car . . . also will be taken to the FBI lab for tests."

Page 62: Joseph put on the breastplate, fastening it with the metal straps around his neck and his waist. Then he fastened the Urim and Thummim to the breastplate, adjusting them like spectacles so they sat before his eyes, leaving his hands free to work. Oliver could see that the frames were made of silver, in the shape of a bow, like an 8 turned sideways—the sign for infinity. Each side of the bow held a transparent crystal in the form of a triangle, one pointing up and the other down. If they were fit together, they would have formed a Star of David. Finally, Joseph removed the cloth that was covering the plates, and for the first time Oliver saw the ancient book.

A popular conception of the translation process has the Prophet and his scribe separated by a curtain, ostensibly so that the scribe would not be able to see the plates. Current scholarship does not support this view, and there probably was no curtain. See, for example, Richard Lyman Bushman, *Joseph Smith: Rough Stone Rolling* (New York, Alfred A. Knopf, 2005), 72.

Pages 62–63: The record was composed of several hundred individual plates, the whole having the appearance of gold, and the plates were held together by three rings, in the shape of a D, running through holes at the edge. Oliver could clearly see the engravings, which were small and beautifully made. The bottom two-thirds of the stack of plates were sealed with a gold band. Joseph had already translated about a dozen of the top third—which translation, he explained, had been lost by Martin Harris. These pages were now turned over face down on the table to the right, with the remaining plates to be translated on the left—exactly the opposite of a book written in English.

These descriptions of the sacred artifacts are based on historical statements from various witnesses. For details, see Matthew B. Brown, *Plates of Gold: The Book of Mormon Comes Forth* (Salt Lake City: Covenant Communications, 2003).

Joseph Smith wrote, "The title page of the Book of Mormon is a literal translation, taken from the very last leaf, on the left hand side of the collection or book of plates, which contained the record which has been translated; the language of the whole running the same as all Hebrew writing in general; and that, said title page is not by any means a modern composition either of mine or of any other man's who has lived or does live in this generation." (*Times and Seasons,* 3:943.)

Page 63: Now he began reading, and as he did so, Oliver began to write, using a goose quill cut with his penknife.

A "penknife" is a knife used to cut the tip of a quill feather (usually from a goose) so it can be used as a pen. People did not simply write with feathers. After the quill was hardened, "a knife was used to slice off the quill end obliquely, exposing the hollow canal inside, which through capillary action became a sort of ink reservoir. The knife then carved a broad edge on the pen, which in turn gave the writing thick or thin strokes, depending on the direction the pen was pushed or pulled. Before writing could begin, however, a tiny slit had to be cut in the tip to allow ink to flow whenever pressure on the page opened the slit." (Michael Olmert, *The Smithsonian Book of Books* [New York: Wings Books, 1992], 73.) In addition, most of the feathering was stripped off to get it out of the way, leaving just the central quill in the hand—contrary to the popular notion often portrayed in movies and television programs. See Christopher de Hamel, *Scribes and Illuminators* [London: British Museum Press, 1992], 27–29.

> *Page 63:* Working clear to the edges so as not to waste the precious paper, he inscribed the words on a small "booklet" of six sheets that he had lined, folded, and sewn together earlier that morning.

Paper was an expensive commodity during Joseph Smith's time, and this is an accurate depiction of how Oliver Cowdery worked. See Royal W. Skousen, ed., *The Original Manuscript of the Book of Mormon: Typographical Facsimile of the Extant Text* [Provo: FARMS, 2001], 34.

> *Page 63:* "And now," the Prophet dictated, "there was no more contention in all the land of Zarahemla among all the people which belonged to King Benjamin . . ."

After the loss of the 116 pages of the Book of Mormon manuscript, Joseph and Oliver probably began translating at the beginning of the book of Mosiah, turning to the small plates of Nephi (1 Nephi through Words of Mormon) only after the rest of the translation was finished. See John W. Welch and Tim Rathbone, "Book of Mormon Translation by Joseph Smith," in Daniel H. Ludlow, ed., *Encyclopedia of Mormonism*, 4 vols. (New York: Macmillan, 1992), 1:210–13;

John W. Welch, "How long did it take Joseph Smith to translate the Book of Mormon?" *Ensign,* January 1988, 46–47.

> *Page 81:* At the other side of the table, Joseph was poised to write, and Oliver haltingly began to dictate: "Yea, in every . . . city . . . throughout all the land . . . which was . . . possessed . . . by the . . . people of Nephi. And it came to pass . . . that they did . . . appoint . . . priests and teachers—"

In the original manuscript of the Book of Mormon, for the single verse of Alma 45:22, the handwriting changes from Oliver Cowdery's to that of Joseph Smith. This may indicate that Oliver translated this verse while Joseph wrote, but it is not conclusive. See Royal W. Skousen, ed., *The Original Manuscript of the Book of Mormon: Typographical Facsimile of the Extant Text* [Provo: FARMS, 2001], 6; also plate 8.

> *Page 92:* Near the north wall of the parking garage, David was standing behind a concrete pillar, trying not to breathe. Thornton was just twenty feet away, fiddling with the latch on a rusty iron door, and David could hear him muttering under his breath. Finally he heard a loud clank, and the door creaked open—and then creaked shut. *Not good,* David thought; he wouldn't be able to reopen the door without Thornton hearing him. Going to the door and putting his ear to the crack in the doorway, he listened as Thornton walked quickly ahead, the footsteps finally fading into silence. He forced himself to wait another full minute, counting off the seconds one by one. Then, with infinite slowness, he opened the door, gritting his teeth and stopping at each tiny squeak.
>
> When the door was open far enough, David squeezed through the crack, leaving the door open. Then he put his hands out, feeling his way along. Concrete walls, but rough this time, not finished. And no fluorescent lights.

As far as I know, there is no hidden stairway or tunnel leading from the Church Office Building to the Daughters of the Utah Pioneers Museum. The door and stairway are figments of my imagination. It is true, however, that from the Church's underground parking garage, one can access the Salt Lake Temple, the Tabernacle, the Assembly Hall, the Church Office Building, the Church Administration Building, the Beehive House, the Joseph Smith Memorial Building, and the Conference Center. (That doesn't mean they'll let you park down there.)

Page 93: The darkness, the silence, were overwhelming. And for the first time in a long time, he prayed. *Please protect me,* he pleaded. *I've been too arrogant, too full of doubt. Watch over me and help me do what I need to do.*

As I wrote this, I had in mind the prayer of the prophet Jonah from the belly of the great fish:

"Then Jonah prayed unto the Lord his God out of the fish's belly, and said, I cried by reason of mine affliction unto the Lord, and he heard me; out of the belly of hell cried I, and thou heardest my voice. For thou hadst cast me into the deep, in the midst of the seas; and the floods compassed me about; all thy billows and thy waves passed over me. Then I said, I am cast out of thy sight; yet I will look again toward thy holy temple.

"The waters compassed me about, even to the soul; the depth closed me round about, the weeds were wrapped about my head. I went down to the bottoms of the mountains; the earth with her bars was about me forever; yet hast thou brought up my life from corruption, O Lord my God. When my soul fainted within me I remembered the Lord; and my prayer came in unto thee, into thine holy temple. They that observe lying vanities forsake their own mercy. But I will sacrifice unto thee with the voice of thanksgiving; I will pay that that I have vowed. Salvation is of the Lord.

"And the Lord spake unto the fish, and it vomited out Jonah upon the dry land." (Jonah 2:1–10.)

> *Page 93:* Nothing changed. But his breathing seemed easier, his pain lighter. He took out his keys and turned on the flashlight. The bulb was dim but steady, and though he couldn't see far, he moved ahead, more cautiously this time, slowly mounting each stair, making his way up through the blackness.

Here I had in mind 1 Nephi 4:5–7: "I Nephi, crept into the city and went forth towards the house of Laban. And I was led by the Spirit, not knowing beforehand the things which I should do. Nevertheless I went forth." I was also thinking of Elder Boyd K. Packer's talk "The Edge of the Light." He said, "Shortly after I was called as a General Authority, I went to Elder Harold B. Lee for counsel. He listened very carefully to my problem and suggested that I see President David O. McKay. President McKay counseled me as to the direction I should go. I was very willing to be obedient but saw no way possible for me to do as he counseled me to do.

"I returned to Elder Lee and told him that I saw no way to move in the direction I was counseled to go. He said, 'The trouble with you is you want to see the end from the beginning.' I replied that I would like to see at least a step or two ahead. Then came the lesson of a lifetime: 'You must learn to walk to the edge of the light, and then a few steps into the darkness; then the light will appear and show the way before you.' Then he quoted these eighteen words from the Book of Mormon: 'Dispute not because ye see not, for ye receive no witness until after the trial of your faith.'

"Those eighteen words from Moroni have been like a beacon light to me." (*BYU Today* 45, no. 2 [March 1991], 38–43.)

Page 96: At the museum he sometimes bumped into Sonny, who especially liked to prowl the back room where the old books and manuscripts were kept, many of them priceless. *Sonny's playground,* he thought. If Sonny went missing from the bookstore, Seth always knew where to find him. Thornton was tempted to go up to the manuscript room himself; maybe he could grab a few things. But he'd never be able to sell them; everything there was too well known. *And besides,* he reminded himself, *that's how I got into this mess.*

The Daughters of the Utah Pioneers Museum in Salt Lake City was the victim of several thefts in April 2006. For more information:

http://findarticles.com/p/articles/mi_qn4188/is_20060 413/ai_n16171615

http://findarticles.com/p/articles/mi_qn4188/is_20060 417/ai_n16162800

http://findarticles.com/p/articles/mi_qn4188/is_20060 415/ai_n16166513

http://deseretnews.com/dn/view/0,1249,635199923, 00.html

The museum, by the way, deserves your interest and support. You can learn about it here:

http://www.dupinternational.org/

Page 101: Seth held the long, heavy cylinder while the officer unwrapped the straw, then, using his pocketknife, cut off a one-inch section. "Now shine it on the fuel filter." With a couple of twists, the officer removed the filter from the gas line and replaced it with the piece of straw. "That won't last long," he said. "You should get a new filter first thing tomorrow. But it will get you up the hill."

"That's amazing," Seth said. "I can't believe how you did that."

The officer beamed with pleasure.

Then Seth clubbed him in the head with the flashlight.

My friends on the police force assure me that no self-respecting officer would ever ask someone to hold a flashlight, since (as in the story) it could be used as a weapon. In addition, although using a soda straw to temporarily replace a fuel filter might work (I haven't tried it, nor should you), it's a really bad idea that could very well lead to the kind of explosion Seth experienced in the story.

Pages 106–7: Thornton looked down at David. He'd actually hit the guy—and hard, too! He was a little surprised at his own strength. But there David was, crumpled up like a paper doll, still as death, his eyes closed. *I hope I didn't kill him,* he thought. He put his hand under David's nose, felt the breath moving in and out. *He's still alive,* he thought. He was glad. Stealing was one thing; killing was another. Then he noticed the gun. Almost against his will, he pulled it out of David's hand. It was heavier than it looked—and it looked enormous. He *really* didn't want to use that. But if he had to, it would be a lot more protection—and a lot more persuasive—than someone's old walking stick. On his way back to the door, he put Brigham Young's cane back into the barrel.

The cane I have in mind is actually in the Museum of Church History and Art rather than the Pioneer Museum, and it's in a display case rather than a barrel.

Page 141: Sagebrush grew around the perimeter, and many of the burial plots were choked with weeds. There was no grass—nor any way to water it if there had been. . . .

The board wasn't much, but his mother couldn't afford a stone, and it looked better than some of the other markers—a piece of sandstone someone had inscribed with a nail, and a rough wooden cross with painted letters.

This is an accurate depiction of the Pleasant Green Cemetery in Magna, Utah, and some of the graves therein.

Page 188: Slowly it dawned on him.

"April," he said, "there are two paragraphs of explanation."

She started to smile. "There are, aren't there."

Latter-day Saint scholar Daniel H. Ludlow suggests that
Mormon may have written the first section of the Title Page,
and Moroni the second. ("The Title Page," *The Book of
Mormon: First Nephi, the Doctrinal Foundation* [Provo:
Religious Studies Center, 1988], 28–31.) If he is correct, that
could explain why the first section of the Anthon Transcript is
written in larger characters than the second section.

See also Sidney B. Sperry, "Moroni the Lonely: The Story
of the Writing of the Title Page to the Book of Mormon,"
Improvement Era 47 (February 1944): 83, 116, 118, reprinted
in *Improvement Era* 73 (November 1970): 110–11. This
article can also be found at:

http://maxwellinstitute.byu.edu/display.php?table=jbms
&id=97

Page 190: After a few minutes of scanning, April said, "I
see that pattern—but it's not in the right place to match the
transcript."

"Maybe that's okay," he said. "What are you looking at?"

"'The gift and power of God,' six lines down, and 'the
gift of God,' at the end of the paragraph."

"Wow," he said. "If that's right, then the circled character
means 'power.'"

This discovery and David's partial translation later in the
book are loosely based on a proposed translation of the
Anthon Transcript by Community of Christ member Blair
Bryant. His impressive work can be seen online here:

http://www.geocities.com/bbbinil/

Page 199: "BYU is working with Oxford University on
ancient documents from Oxyrhynchus, and they're reading

Greek and Latin scrolls that were carbonized during the eruption of Mount Vesuvius. The documents are completely black, but they can read them."

This is true. For more information, see:
http://newsnet.byu.edu/story.cfm/55780
There's another interesting article about this in the *Washington Post,* May 30, 2005, A08. The article is available online here:
http://www.washingtonpost.com/wp-dyn/content/article/2005/05/29/AR2005052900811_pf.html

Page 199: David watched with amazement as John Shafer, from the university's engineering department, showed him how the multispectral imager worked. Using a test document written with two kinds of ink, he changed the part of the spectrum by which the document was viewed. At first, David didn't see anything different. But as John continued to change the light wavelength, gradually the writing in one kind of ink faded out, while the writing in the other kind became darker, easier to read.

You can see an online example of how this works at POxy:
http://www.papyrology.ox.ac.uk/POxy/multi/index.html

Page 200: "It's a postscript from Joseph Smith—in code."

Joseph Smith did sometimes add postscripts to his letters. For examples, see *The Personal Writings of Joseph Smith,* rev. ed., edited by Dean C. Jessee (Salt Lake City: Deseret Book, 2002), 260, 408.

Pages 202, 211: In reading this, you should not suppose the translation was not of God, for it was given by His gift and power through the medium of the Urim and Thummim, the particulars of which are not for the world to know. I pray this explains my imposture regarding the seerstone.

I based this statement on a passage from Joseph Smith's *History of the Church*, 1:220: "Brother Hyrum Smith said that he thought best that the information of the coming forth of the Book of Mormon be related by Joseph himself to the Elders present, that all might know for themselves.

"Brother Joseph Smith, Jun., said that it was not intended to tell the world all the particulars of the coming forth of the Book of Mormon; and also said that it was not expedient for him to relate these things."

See appendix B, "Seerstones."

Pages 204–5: "Elder Pratt wrote, 'When Sidney Rigdon was through, brother Joseph arose like a lion about to roar; and being full of the Holy Ghost, spoke in great power, bearing testimony of the visions he had seen, the ministering of angels which he had enjoyed.'"

This story, here slightly modified, comes from Parley P. Pratt, *The Autobiography of Parley P. Pratt* (Salt Lake City: Deseret Book, 1938), 298–99. It's a great book, well worth reading, and has been reprinted numerous times.

APPENDIX A: THE STONE BOX

꒣ ≋ ┼┤

Oliver Cowdery wrote the following description of the stone box in a letter to William W. Phelps:

The manner in which the plates were deposited:

First, a hole of sufficient depth, (how deep I know not,) was dug. At the bottom of this was laid a stone of suitable size, the upper surface being smooth. At each edge was placed a large quantity of cement, and into this cement, at the four edges of this stone, were placed, erect, four others, *their* bottom edges resting *in* the cement at the outer edges of the first stone. The four last named, when placed erect, formed a box, the corners, or where the edges of the four came in contact, were also cemented so firmly that the moisture from without was prevented from entering. It is to be observed, also, that the inner surface of the four erect, or side stones was smooth. This box was sufficiently large to admit a breast-plate, such as was used by the ancients to defend the chest, &c., from the arrows and weapons of their enemy. From the bottom of the box, or from the breast-plate, arose three small pillars composed of the same description of cement used on the edges; and upon these three pillars was placed the record of the children of Joseph, and of a people who left the tower far, far before the days of Joseph, or a sketch of each. . . .

I must not forget to say that this box, containing the record was covered with another stone, the bottom surface being flat and the upper, crowning. But those three pillars were not so lengthy as to cause the plates and the crowning stone to come in contact. (*Messenger and Advocate,* vol. 2, no. 1 [October 1835]: 196.)

In 1875 a newspaper reporter who interviewed David Whitmer wrote, "Three times has he been at the hill Cumorah and seen the casket that contained the tablets and the seerstone [Urim and Thummim]. Eventually the casket had been washed down to the foot of the hill, but it was to be seen when he last visited the historic place." (*Chicago Times,* August 7, 1875, in Lyndon W. Cook, ed., *David Whitmer Interviews: A Restoration Witness* (Orem, Utah: Grandin, 1991), 7.

John Landers (1794–1892) told this story:

We heard the first sound of the restored gospel through my wife's brother, John Cairns, who had been baptized by Father Blakeslee. John preached one sermon to us, and I believed what he preached to be the truth, and told him so. Some time after, a traveling elder came that way, and I went to hear him preach. At the close of his sermon he bore a strong testimony to the truth of the work, and holding up the three books—Bible, Book of Mormon, and Doctrine and Covenants—he testified that he knew them to be all sacred, and that they all agreed in teaching the same doctrine.

After the service I invited the man home with me, and he went. One of my first questions was, "How can you say you know these books are true?"

He answered by relating to me how he had seen a vision concerning the plates, and when he had finished I said, "Well, that may be satisfactory to you, but your knowledge will not suffice for me. If I had such a vision, I should know." He rose and advanced to me, saying, "I want to prophesy upon your head," and laying his hands upon my head, he prophesied that I should have as great, as certain a knowledge, as he had.

I heard him preach four discourses, and while listening to the fourth, the Spirit of the Lord bore witness that he was the servant of God and that it was my duty to obey. I was baptized on the seventh day of October 1836.

A conference was called in November and I was ordained an elder. I immediately formed a circuit and began to travel, preaching every night. My nephew, a young man, traveled and labored with me. One night we had appointed a meeting at a private house. After the meeting was closed, a man came to me and asked me how this doctrine that I was preaching came into the world, and I told him in response all that I had been told concerning it and the origin of the Book of Mormon. The man sat down beside me, and just then my brother's son arose and began speaking in tongues, and immediately I was carried away in vision and stood on the hill of Cumorah.

I looked and saw the box containing the plates. I stood at the southeast of the box, and the cover was removed from the southeast to the northwest corner, so that I was enabled to look into the box. The box was made of six stones, a bottom stone, a top one and four side stones; at the corners and edges they were joined by a black cement. The bottom of the box was covered by the breastplate; in the center of the box and resting on the breastplate, were three pillars of the same black substance that was used to cement the stones.

Upon the pillars rested the plates which shone like bright gold. I saw also lying in the box a round body, wrapped in a white substance, and this I knew to be the ball or directors which so many years ago guided Lehi and his family to this land. The top stone of the box was smooth on the inner surface as were the others, but on the top it was rounded.

All this was described by the young man speaking in tongues, and as he talked I understood all he said, for I saw it in the vision. Thus was fulfilled the prophecy that had been pronounced upon my head, and the Spirit of the Lord said to me that this had been granted me that I might speak with certain knowledge when questioned concerning the origin of the Book of Mormon and the latter day work. ("A Vision of the Gold Plates of the Book of Mormon," *Autumn Leaves* [periodical; Independence, Mo.: The Reorganized Church of Jesus Christ of Latter Day Saints], 3:68.)

APPENDIX B: SEERSTONES

꓿ ≋ ㅓ

In this novel, I contend that Joseph and Oliver used the Urim and Thummim rather than a seerstone to translate the Book of Mormon. I base this on their own statements and on the fact that any assertions to the contrary were made many years later by people not directly involved in the translation as Joseph and Oliver were. The Book of Mormon itself consistently refers to the "interpreters," or Urim and Thummim:

> Now Ammon said unto him: I can assuredly tell thee, O king, of a man that can translate the records; for he has wherewith that he can look, and translate all records that are of ancient date; and it is a gift from God. And the things are called interpreters, and no man can look in them except he be commanded, lest he should look for that he ought not and he should perish. And whosoever is commanded to look in them, the same is called seer. And behold, the king of the people who are in the land of Zarahemla is the man that is commanded to do these things, and who has this high gift from God. (Mosiah 8:3–14.)

> And now he translated them by the means of those two stones which were fastened into the two rims of a bow. Now these things were prepared from the beginning, and were handed down from generation to generation, for the purpose of interpreting languages; and they have been kept and

preserved by the hand of the Lord, that he should discover to every creature who should possess the land the iniquities and abominations of his people; and whosoever has these things is called seer, after the manner of old times. (Mosiah 28:13–16.)

And now, my son, these interpreters were prepared that the word of God might be fulfilled, which he spake, saying: I will bring forth out of darkness unto light all their secret works and their abominations; and except they repent I will destroy them from off the face of the earth; and I will bring to light all their secrets and abominations, unto every nation that shall hereafter possess the land. (Alma 37:24–25.)

President Joseph Fielding Smith wrote, "While the statement has been made by some writers that the Prophet Joseph Smith used a seer stone part of the time in his translating of the record, and information points to the fact that he did have in his possession such a stone, yet there is no authentic statement in the history of the Church which states that the use of such a stone was made in that translation. The information is all hearsay, and personally, I do not believe that this stone was used for this purpose. The reason I give for this conclusion is found in the statement of the Lord to the Brother of Jared as recorded in Ether 3:22–24." (Joseph Fielding Smith, *Doctrines of Salvation*, 3 vols., edited by Bruce R. McConkie [Salt Lake City: Bookcraft, 1954–1956], 3:225.)

The reference in Ether that Elder Smith referred to reads as follows:

And behold, when ye shall come unto me, ye shall write them and shall seal them up, that no one can interpret them; for ye shall write them in a language that they cannot be read. And behold, these two stones will I give unto thee, and ye shall seal them up also with the things which ye shall write. For behold, the language which ye shall write I have confounded; wherefore I will cause in my own due time that

239

these stones shall magnify to the eyes of men these things which ye shall write. And when the Lord had said these words, he showed unto the brother of Jared all the inhabitants of the earth which had been, and also all that would be; and he withheld them not from his sight, even unto the ends of the earth. (Ether 3:22–25.)

Joseph Smith's possible use of a seerstone in translating has been described many times in official Church publications, including:

B. H. Roberts, "The Probability of Joseph Smith's Story," *Improvement Era,* March 1904.

Richard Lloyd Anderson, "'By the Gift and Power of God,'" *Ensign,* September 1977.

Kenneth W. Godfrey, "A New Prophet and a New Scripture: The Coming Forth of the Book of Mormon," *Ensign,* January 1988.

Russell M. Nelson, "A Treasured Testament," *Ensign,* July 1993.

Neal A. Maxwell, "By the Gift and Power of God," *Ensign,* January 1997.

More information can be found here:

Daniel C. Peterson, "The Divine Source of the Book of Mormon in the Face of Alternative Theories Advocated by LDS Critics," which is found at:

http://www.fairlds.org/FAIR_Conferences/2001_Divine _Source_of_the_Book_of_Mormon_in_the_Face_of_Alternativ e_Theories.html

Stephen D. Ricks, "Translation of the Book of Mormon: Interpreting the Evidence," *Journal of Book of Mormon Studies,* Volume 2, Issue 2, which is found at:

http://farms.byu.edu/display.php?table=jbms&id=41

ACKNOWLEDGMENTS

This book could not have been published without the help of many people. I offer my gratitude to Bill Slaughter and Ron Watt at the Historical Department of The Church of Jesus Christ of Latter-day Saints; Edith Menna at the Daughters of the Utah Pioneers Memorial Museum; and Jana Erickson, Emily Watts, Anne Sheffield, Richard Peterson, Lisa Mangum, Shauna Gibby, and Laurie Cook at Deseret Book—each of whom made a contribution to this novel. In particular, I'd like to thank Jay Parry, my editor at Deseret Book, for his insightful suggestions, good humor, and steadfast friendship. I'd like to thank Yvonne Lyon (my daughter-in-law) for giving me Thornton's last name, Roy Orton and Claron Brenchley for answering my questions about police procedure, and Rob Anderson (my son-in-law) and Wayne Williams (my brother-in-law) for answering my questions about firearms. I'd also like to thank my dad and mom (Glade and Katie, who gave me my love of books), my wonderful wife (Anne), my spectacular kids (Rebekah, John, Matthew, and Rachel), and my terrific sisters (Suzanne, Robin, and Kathy).

ABOUT THE AUTHOR

⇉ ≋ ⊢

Jack Lyon, previously managing editor at Deseret Book, is a writer and publisher, the owner of Waking Lion Press and Temple Hill Books. His publications include *Best-Loved Stories of the LDS People*, *Best-Loved Humor of the LDS People*, *The Ultimate Guide to GospeLink*, *Managing the Obvious*, and several other books. At Deseret Book, he edited the *Children of the Promise* and *Hearts of the Children* novels by Dean Hughes, *The Collected Works of Hugh Nibley*, and *The Papers of Joseph Smith*, along with hundreds of other publications during a career of more than twenty-five years. In the Church, he serves as a Gospel Doctrine teacher. He and his wife, Anne, live in West Valley City, Utah. They have four children and five grandchildren.

.